I, CLAUDIA

I, CLAUDIA

A Novel of the Ancient World

Lin Wilder

ALSO BY LIN WILDER

A Search For the Sacred

Finding the Narrow Path

The Fragrance Shed by a Violet

Do You Solemnly Swear?

A Price for Genius

Malthus Revisited

I, Claudia: A Novel of the Ancient World
Lin Wilder

ISBN: 978-1-948018-43-2
Library of Congress Control Number: 2018914485

Temple of Hephaestus, Athens, Greece ©CAHKT | iStockPhoto
Woman in cloak praying © Nejron | Dreamstime.comt

Wilder Books
An Imprint of Wyatt-MacKenzie

DEDICATION

To those rare searchers for Truth:
Courage and Persistence

Knowledge has three degrees: opinion, science, illumination.
The means of instrument of the first is senses, the second,
dialectic; the third, intuition.
—PLOTINUS

The greatest blessings come by way of madness, indeed of
madness that is heaven-sent.
—SOCRATES ON THE ORACLE AT DELPHI

While he was sitting on the judgment seat, his wife sent him
a message, saying, "Have nothing to do with that righteous
Man; for last night I suffered greatly in a dream
because of Him."
—GOSPEL OF MATTHEW, 27:19

The 21ˢᵗ-century Christian will be either a "mystic," that is,
a person who has "experienced" something,
or he will not be a Christian.
—KARL RAHNER

PROLOGUE

They wore the faces of my dreams. Men, women, and children, mouths open in joyous shouts, made soundless by the din of hundreds of marching feet. The people lined the narrow streets, the wealthier watching from their palace rooftops, their children tossing brightly colored scarves upon the phalanxes of soldiers. The lead centurion held the shield of Tiberius steadily aloft: S.P.Q.R. *Senātus Populusque Rōmānus* (Roman Senate and People). The legionnaire moved it only when an errant puff of color landed on the scarlet standard, momentarily obscuring the golden eagle glittering in the bright sunlight.

He has had his arms raised for how many hours now?
Shouldn't there be a Joshua to help this Moses?

I suppressed a smile at my wittiness, knowing better than to voice the thought aloud. My ladies would be shocked by my allusion to the great Jewish prophet. I was well aware of my reputation as an empty-headed nitwit among those who served my husband; such low expectations had served me well. Best to maintain the fiction.

Soft pinks, yellows, reds, and blues of all shades drifted lazily down the still, hot currents of desert air. They resembled butterflies until our carriage drew close enough to see that they were scarves. Some of the soft cloths puddled on the dirt streets as I watched, only to be trampled by the next column of tightly grouped soldiers. The morning sun made the helmets and shields of the marching men radiate so brightly that they could not be looked at without squinting. I closed my eyes tightly against the glare, wishing vainly that the familiar faces of the onlookers were just another dream; terrified that when I opened them, I would see those same faces filled with hatred, their mouths joining in the monstrous roar of malevolence, commanding the death of the righteous one.

"M'lady, M'lady, are you all right?" I could hear Antonia's concern. She knew how I had dreaded this journey, how fervent had been my prayers for some miracle to forestall what I knew was destiny—his, mine, and the world's. Unlike the others, Antonia had known me almost since birth.

"I'm fine, Antonia, fine. Please do not worry, I am just drained. We have been traveling now for more than thirty days. The heat makes it almost impossible to sleep at night—it never cools off here."

It was still only midmorning, and yet the temperature had to be over ninety. The fall weather in Athens had always been gloriously cool, crisp, wholly different from this unrelenting, insufferable heat.

Antonia wasn't fooled by my reply, in spite of my attempt at a smile. I did not blame her. I knew that the upturn of my lips was more rictus than smile...and with good reason. We were heading toward a doom of the kind the world had never seen, and I knew there was nothing I could do or say to stop it. Surveying my surroundings, I felt no relief at the unchanged jubilance, the joyous expressions on the faces of the crowds.

It would come, and soon.

I am nearing the end of my life. Seventy-nine years lived as a shadow, a face behind a curtain, whispering the residues of a dream. Insubstantial, unheard. But my time of silence is done.

It is time to write the truth for those with ears to hear it.

I am Procula, wife of Lucius Pontius Pilate. My husband has been dead for several decades now. Like me, Lucius is the subject of vast ignorance, lies, and injustice. The very name *Pontius Pilate* has become synonymous with cowardice and betrayal.

Those who claim to know the substance of my dream believe it emanates from evil. Others insist that those words that will be recited by Christians, "Suffered under Pontius Pilate, was crucified, and died," were the source of terror in my dreams. I was told by the Oracle that those eight words would echo throughout the centuries and be memorialized in something that would be called the Apostles' Creed. Most of the people reciting the Creed would mindlessly overlook the word *under* and believe that the Righteous One was crucified *by* my husband.

The slanderous claims, and all others like them, no longer break my heart; they are merely annoying. I often think of the writing of Socrates, a man I consider a good friend though he died before I was born. His wisdom and humility await those rare searchers of truth. "I know I am intelligent because I know I know nothing."

I was born in Delphi, daughter of the last of the Oracles of Pythia. It was a time of disorder, chaos, terror, and the death of nations. My mother broke her vow of virginity in lying with my father. She feared for both our lives, because what she had done was punishable by death—hers and mine. The time of the Oracles was coming to an end. Men no longer listened to the whispers of the prophets, certainly not to the women—not even when we had the words of the gods on our lips.

I survived, but my mother did not. I was taken to Athens, where I was raised by Adrian and Sabina. Only they knew that I was the last Oracle; my true identity remained a secret to all others—although my husband speculated as much, due to my foreknowledge of so many things.

I ask that you permit a conceit. This book will be told in

two voices: my own and my husband's. Perhaps that seems presumptuous, or worse: specious? My defense is this: Near the end of his life, almost daily, my husband told me that I knew him better than he knew himself. He talked incessantly about how close he had come to refusing the thunderous command of the Jews. When Quintillus, Lucius's best friend and peerless centurion, gave me Lucius's *Final Report of Lucius Pontius Pilate to Tiberius Caesar on the Crucifixion of the Christ*, including the letters he'd exchanged with Seneca, this book designed itself.

Could I have intervened when the famed Stoic philosopher directed my husband's every thought? Incited a hatred toward the Jews that cost him and the world—no less than everything?

You decide.

CHAPTER ONE

ATHENS, MACEDONIA
Claudia Procula

They say it is impossible. I was, after all, barely two when we left Greece. But I remember Delphi. The only place I knew as home echoes in my mind and heart still, after almost eight decades of absence. The Delphian air is purer, the sky bluer, and the mountains redolent with wisdom. Scrambling through the tunnels beneath the Treasury of Athena kept me safer than I'd have been in a nanny's arms, and infused me with more knowledge than did my later tutors. It was there, crawling alone around and under those sacred stone structures, that the unreliability of the senses, the language of the Forms, the highest Good, transcendent and absolute, impressed themselves into my very being. That there was just one god, not many, was a certainty I shared with the Hebrews.

Too young. It's absurd. Inconceivable.

I know. I think that too, as I write this so many years later. But the truth is this. By the time I was nine, my Aunt Sabina and Uncle Adrian—my kind, adoptive parents—decided I was old enough to study philosophy, mathematics, rhetoric, Latin, and Greek. Sabina hired tutors, the best in Athens. She could not

1

understand why they lasted just days.

"Claudia Procula! Alejandro has quit," she admonished me. "He is the third tutor you've had in three months. I had to pay him a month's wages though he was here for only five days!"

I looked up from the scroll of Plato's *Republic*. Sabina stood looking down at me, her expression a mixture of puzzlement and something else—I wasn't sure what. Without thinking, I retorted, "You and Uncle Adrian could have saved a substantial sum if you had listened when I asked to spend my days in the Aristotle Library."

The color in her cheeks rising, Sabina visibly worked to control her anger. She was Mother's older sister by ten years and must have been past forty, but her beauty remained. She wore a dark-violet stola with a light-lavender shawl tied at her narrow waist with a gold braid. A gold armband served as her only jewelry. Sabina had competed in the Heraean Games twice and won laurel crowns each time in the long-distance marathons. Her shape had changed little since those days.

Touching her long, blonde braid, my aunt's expression and voice softened as she studied me. "Why do these men quit tutoring you, Claudia? What makes them want to leave so suddenly? Alejandro could not remove himself from here fast enough. It was almost as if he thought you—" Abruptly, she covered her mouth momentarily, then let her slender hand drop back to her side. She closed her eyes and murmured the prayer I had heard often since childhood.

"Clear-eyed Athena, unrivaled in wisdom, daughter of Zeus and Metis whose craft and wit excelled among the mighty Titans: Athena, I pray to you. Wise in all things you are, goddess;your cunning and guile are well known. In time of war you have no equal in tactics or in strategy; many armies have you guided to victory. In time of peace your blessings fall on those whose work is of the mind–friend of the philosopher, the scientist, the student. Advisor of kings, patron of clever heroes and bold-hearted adventurers, defender of the thinker, mistress of reason and understanding, goddess to whom a strong arm and a sharp sword are nothing without the sense to wield them well and the insight to know when words are worth more than weapons. Athena, grant me a sound mind and steady temper, bless me with good judgment, show me the long view."

"These words are beautiful, even wise, Aunt Sabina, but Athena is just an illusion. Her mouth produces no words, her mind no thoughts, and her heart does not beat. Your goddess is merely an instrument on which to hang human weakness."

The moment the words came out of my mouth, I wanted to reach into the still, warm, summer air, grab them and eat them.

My aunt swayed ever so slightly from side to side, her turquoise eyes hardening into flint. "You have no right! With all of her gifts—the gifts you share—your mother *never...ever...* spoke so cruelly. Know this, Claudia Procula: Should you utter one more viperous word, you will be out of this house!" Impossibly, her eyes grew even colder. "Someone as wise as you surely knows what would become of an abandoned female ten-year-old, does she not?"

I learned on that sultry afternoon just how massive a burden it was to possess the supernatural knowledge I had done nothing to merit. I also learned that once loathsome, pitiless words are uttered, no power in this world or another can cauterize the wounds they make. They bleed into eternity.

CHAPTER TWO

GERMANIA
Lucius Pontius Pilate

I was born to be a warrior. Until I donned the tunic, body armor, and shoulder plates of the legionnaire, I felt like a child. I knew upon grabbing the dagger, sword, javelin, and shield that this was my destiny. As a boy, I had been ungainly, all angles, awkward and fumbling. But as I placed the helmet on my head and joined my legion, I knew that time had passed. I would lead men. And soon.

The march from Rome to the outskirts of Germanicus was dreadful. Our commander underestimated the effect of the northern winter and overestimated the strength and endurance of his legion. More than one hundred Roman soldiers died from exposure and exhaustion before we met a single Germanian. Stupidity. Incompetence. Inexcusable in a leader. My pent-up anger when we finally met our enemy whipped my speed, tactics, and deadliness into something manic, crazed, unstoppable. At the end of that first day, exhausted and improperly clothed, we sent the Germans fleeing. The Roman soldiers who had survived were cheering my name.

"LUCIUS!"

"PONTIUS!"

"PILATE!"

Our Tribune was dead. Overnight, at the age of twenty-eight, I became Tribune.

Was it destiny that caused Tiberius to ride onto the blood-soaked German soil just as the men were hauling me atop their shoulders and shouting my name? Was it fate that caused the next emperor of Rome to smile as he replaced my helmet with a laurel wreath? As he wordlessly crowned me Tribune after my very first day of battle, the men continued shouting my three names until the trees shook.

Had I known Claudia then, and had she told me of my future, would I have turned away from my calling, cutting short my rapid ascent to the pinnacle of the best army the world had ever witnessed? Could I have become a farmer like my brother... a physician like my uncle...or perhaps a consul like Seneca?

Seneca, he to whom I gave my trust blindly. He whose words I revered and whose viewpoints became mine.

CHAPTER THREE

ATHENS, MACEDONIA
Claudia Procula

At fifteen, I was of marriageable age. Old, even, when compared to the three daughters of Aunt Sabina's best friend Phoebe, all of whom were married by their twelfth birthdays. Girls were expensive and dowries were expected; the wealthier the household, the more extravagant the dowry.

Had Uncle Adrian not been so fond of me, I'd have been gone that dreadful summer afternoon when I stupidly and cruelly insulted Sabina's faith, her goddess Athena. There is no excuse for the lack of respect I showed a woman who had taken me in and done her very best to prepare me for the world.

And yet, when I look back through these ancient eyes, I have sympathy for that impossibly young girl who had just mastered Plato's *Republic*. She'd been feeling the supreme joy of deciphering a map to wisdom, discovering that philosophy can be a practical guide to life.

At the end of that first reading of the *Republic*, I finally had the words to express portions of the inchoate knowledge with which I'd been infused at Delphi: *virtue, justice, immortality, eternity, nobility.* I knew, even then, that there were just two paths: that of the foolish and that of the wise. But the maps delineating those paths were often obscured, even deceptive. I understood that the knowledge of how to live emanates from wisdom—but also that it takes considerable work and study to embody true good. The pursuit of wisdom would assure that I would not live the life of the fool.

Upon reading Socrates' explication of Plato for the first time, I didn't just learn but *recognized* the writer's words:

> *That the true lover of knowledge is always striving after being—that is his nature; he will not rest in the multiplicity of individuals which is an appearance only, but will go on—the keen edge will not be blunted, nor the force of his desire abate until he have attained the knowledge of the true nature of every essence by a sympathetic and kindred power in the soul, and by that power drawing near and mingling and becoming incorporate with very being, having begotten mind and truth, he will have knowledge and will live and grow truly, and then, and not till then, will he cease from his travail.*

This was the work of a lifetime—I knew it even then. An endeavor that requires no less than *everything*; a practice that can be shared with no one but the creator.

Uncle Adrian walked in the house just as I was finishing the ninth chapter. "What are you doing, *Claudiaki mou?*" he asked.

Adrian was an aristocrat—one of the *arostoi*—and he looked the part as he stood in the courtyard smiling down at me, the tanned olive skin of his arms and muscular, robust legs contrasting sharply with the gold linen chiton he wore. His distinctive white-wool toga indicated that he had been at the agora that morning.

Due to the force of my concentration, I had not noticed the onset of dusk until I heard his voice. He looked pleased, even relaxed. The morning meeting must have gone well. I knew he had been concerned about the fate of a new tax plan he'd devised with two other citizens. A wealthy property owner, my uncle was an influential citizen in Athens. His was one of the largest farms in Athens, with acres of olive trees and vineyards and more than forty slaves to work it.

"I'm finishing Plato's *Republic*, Uncle," I answered him, proudly pointing at the thick pile of pages I'd read, next to the thin sheaf still to be completed.

Eyebrows raised, his smile grew wide. "This calls for a celebration! Where is Sabina?"

"At Phoebe's. They are working to complete a wedding dress for her youngest daughter."

Reaching down to pull me up off the couch, my uncle said, "Come! Let's find Antonia and some wine. Then you can tell me all that you have learned."

And so I did, for over two hours, as Uncle Adrian listened carefully and asked a question now and then to get me to clarify a point. He was particularly interested in my excitement about the ideal state, the philosopher king, and what I called the "irrefutable logic" of there being just *one* god, not many. Just one cause of everything.

Eyes shining, Uncle Adrian said, "I'm very proud of you, Claudia. When I gave you my copy of those scrolls for your birthday last year, I had no idea that you would devour their content as if it were mere air!"

I think it was the fact that my erudite uncle had seemed to agree with my ideas—even about religion—that inspired the hubris in me and impelled me to correct Sabina. After my foolish outburst, my aunt distanced herself from me entirely and permanently. I faced each successive birthday with increasing apprehension, knowing that the day would soon come when I would be told whom I would marry.

It was a relief then, on the April evening of my fifteenth year, when she appeared in my doorway and said, "Claudia, Adrian and I have decided it is time for you to meet your future husband, Lucius. We'll be leaving early Friday morning. Pack all of your things." She spoke softly from the open door of my room and looked at me warily as if expecting an outburst.

I smiled and stood. "Will you come in and sit for just a moment, Aunt Sabina?" I held my breath. For the past five years, I had tried and failed to have a conversation I hoped desperately now to have.

We stared at one another at eye level. I was now as tall as she, five-foot-seven. I noted a shimmer of surprise in her eyes as, almost unwillingly, my aunt noted the similarity of our bodies. She was lovely, ageless, her skin like porcelain. I could easily see why my uncle had fallen in love with her. Her use of kohl around her eyes was artful, just bold enough to emphasize the unusual shade of them. The red ochre on her lips looked natural. *Was this how my mother looked?* I wondered. Then, with a jolt, *Am I this beautiful?*

I reined in my silly thoughts. *Claudia, you will never have this chance again. Act. Now.*

"Please," I said, holding out my hand. I exhaled softly as she stepped over the threshold of my room and took it.

Sitting on the *kline* I had slept on since a baby, I patted the space next to me.

She sat down, looking as surprised as I was that we were sitting side by side.

"Thank you," I said, turning my body so I could look into those lovely eyes. I knew that in just two days, I would never see her again. "There is no excuse for what I said to you that day, the pain I inflicted with my rash words. Please know how profoundly I regret them. There has not been one day since that I have not felt sorrow and remorse."

Sabina's cheeks flushed, the unbidden shame, the humiliation and most likely anger of that day inflaming them. Her lips parted, and she placed her hands on either side of her thighs—about to bolt, I feared.

Grabbing the hand closest to me, I whispered again, "Please, Aunt, hear me out. Give me a mere five minutes."

I hated the sound of my own begging, but the need to speak the words that had been searing my heart for five years was like a living thing with shape, weight, and dimension. Feeling Sabina's hand relax, I rashly fell to my knees in front of her. "You must know that I will never use my gifts to harm another. Please, dearest sister of my dear mother, you, who opened your home and heart to this orphan, please know how much my heart aches over those impulsively uttered words. Please accept my gratitude for taking me in and allowing me to attain the education I so desired."

Staring at her, I could feel the weight of my own unshed tears, then feel their tracks as they overflowed and slowly descended my face. "Please forgive me."

She rose. The kiss she planted on the crown of my head was a blessing. Her strong arms pulled me up beside her until, once again, we were gazing at each other.

"I do forgive you, Claudia. I do." Her eyes searched mine as if looking for something lost. Then as she clasped me to her bosom, "Your problem, my child, is the oldest in the world. The wisdom you seek so desperately will only disappoint you. It will never be enough. The only true wisdom is in knowing you know nothing."

It would be years before I would realize that my Aunt Sabina had been quoting Socrates. That the woman in whose home I had lived for twelve years was a total stranger.

CHAPTER FOUR

ROME, PALACE OF TIBERIUS
Lucius Pontius Pilate

I waited for hours that steaming August day. Clad in my full Tribune regalia, I must have lost ten pounds in sweat as I awaited Tiberius's summons into his private chambers. My heart pounded, not just from the heat but from a powerful foreboding that my days as a legionnaire were over. The note on the wax tablet had said nothing other than, "Come see me immediately." Tiberius had not even bothered to add his seal.

The journey back to Rome had been exhausting—filled with sporadic fighting with Germanian soldiers who had refused to accept defeat. The passage had taken thirteen days instead of the usual week; I dared not calculate the number of days we'd gone without sleep.

Caesar Augustus, the god-like leader of the Roman Empire, was dying—but he had been close to death for several years. No one was sure just who would be the next Caesar. His succession was thrown into turmoil with the deaths of his grandsons, Lucius and Gaius, after the banishment of their younger brother, Agrippa Postumus, ten years earlier. But this was Roman politics. Nothing was assured until Augustus was dead.

Tiberius was a warrior, like me. We had "recognized" each other during that first blood-soaked battle six years before. As I waited, I deliberated about this man I had come to admire as a leader. Tiberius was a born soldier. Neither subtlety, deception, nor fawning blemished his character—although all three qualities and more were essential if one was to thrive in the boiling cauldron of Roman politics. Although I knew that his ascendancy to Princeps would have a dramatic effect on me and my own career, for the life of me, I could not imagine Tiberius as Caesar. Mainly because he had told me that his was not an authentic claim to the legacy. The great leader of the fading Roman Republic had adopted Tiberius upon the deaths of his own beloved sons, Gaius and Lucius Caesar. Tiberius was a son not by blood but by default. True, he had been quite drunk the night he shared this secret with me, but I believed the truth of it....

That strange confession had emerged after the Germanian victory in the Teutoburg Forest. The cleverly planned ambush by the German tribal leader Arminius had caught Varus, Tiberius's replacement in Germania, by complete surprise and resulted in a rout: four brutal, storm-filled days described more accurately as a massacre than a battle. Tiberius and I, the newly minted legionnaire Tribune, Lucius Pontius Pilate, had arrived in time to view the carnage: More than 15,000 dead Roman legionnaires, along with many of the women and children who had accompanied them on their journey through the "peaceful Roman territory."

It was when we happened upon Varus's body on the bloodsoaked ground, his hands still clutching the spear that impaled his chest, that Tiberius won my lifelong fidelity. We had been carefully picking our way through the corpses, Tiberius astride his pure white Arabian, oblivious to the stench, flies, and hellishness surrounding us. I had no idea what we searched for. The only sounds were those of the horses' hooves as they laboriously sought safe ground free of limbs and bodies. Unconsciously, I sought to imitate my superior, maintain my composure, and keep the contents of my stomach where it belonged.

Abruptly, Tiberius reined in his horse. The gelding snorted in surprise but stopped, and Tiberius instantly dismounted. Without thinking, I followed suit and stood beside him where he knelt...belatedly realizing that the body before us was the Tribune Varus himself.

Where a lesser man may well have given no thought to proper battlefield burial for a leader who'd suffered such an inglorious death, Tiberius gently, almost reverently, picked up the body and assigned four soldiers the task of burying him. Then he turned to me and growled, "I hope you can hold your liquor, young man. Because we're going to get exceedingly drunk."

After several hours of drinking Germanian beer, we were both so inebriated that all self-control was lost. Several times, Tiberius swore he would go into exile rather than accept the laurel crown of the Roman Empire.

I had never been as drunk, even during the early days of legionnaire training when we'd run close to thirty-six kilometers a day, loaded down by thirty-five-and-a-half kilograms of armor. Oh, the impossible feats they demanded of us! All we did was run... and then drink.

Tiberius as Emperor of the Holy Roman Empire? Why, it would be precisely like me becoming a politician...wouldn't it?

I smiled at the memories, even of that swill Posca—the only wine that we could afford. And reveled in my recollection of the grandeur and glory of becoming a Roman legionnaire—the acme of all fighting forces in the world. But my smile faded with the memory of reading the message from Tiberius, and the sense of foreboding that accompanied it.

Suddenly the enormous wooden doors of the inner chambers exploded outward. A phalanx of soldiers stepped out in a tight formation, revealing Sejanus. He was no longer clothed in the uniform of the legionnaire but in a toga and unarmed.

Sejanus is Prefect of the Praetorian Guard, I thought. *By Jove, Augustus must be dead and Tiberius now the Emperor of the Holy Roman Empire!*

Some 753 years ago, after killing his brother Remus, Romulus had personally yoked a bull and a heifer to a plow and marked off the sacred boundaries of his city of Rome. There was no temple to Mars, the god of war, and even generals changed to civilian clothes when they entered the holy precinct. All Roman soldiers knew—even most citizens—that the Palatine Hill was a place of peace, the *pomerium*.

Despite the heat, Lucius felt a chill, as if a cold breeze had materialized. Saying nothing, he merely stared at Sejanus and waited.

CHAPTER FIVE

ATHENS, MACEDONIA
Claudia Procula

"I forbid it. It would be far too dangerous—for my men and me, never mind for you and Claudia! That territory is still riddled with bandits."

I had never heard Uncle Adrian raise his voice, let alone shout. Aunt Sabina's reply was too quiet for me to hear from the doorway of my room on the second floor, where I strained to listen to them talking down in the *andron*. It was by far the largest room in the house and was on the far side from my room—but not so far that my uncle's deep voice did not carry clearly through the still morning air. I knew they were in the space Adrian kept for seeing business associates and hosting important social occasions. I had seen Sabina in there only a few times, when her hospitality to the leaders of Athens was warranted.

Clearly, they did not want me to hear their conversation. I could only conclude that they were talking about me. But what could they be having words about? Soon, I would be gone from their lives and no longer their concern. Whatever the matter, it had surely been raised by Sabina, and was obviously the cause of great consternation for Adrian. His last phrase echoed in my mind: *That territory is still riddled with bandits. Too dangerous even for my men and me....*

I continued to stand silent and alert but could make out nothing further. My things were all packed: Three large woven bags held my clothes and another two, along with a beautifully carved wooden chest, my dowry. I knew the contents. Sabina had been working for weeks on a collection of undergarments for my wedding night and the nights thereafter. Of a variety of pale violets and amber hues, the garments were lovely. There was also a leather satchel that contained a very large sum of money in both Greek and Roman coins.

The dowry. Sabina had offered more than a few times to explain how and why my soon-to-be husband's proposal had been accepted. With each of her attempts to discuss the matter, I had feigned indifference, but I could tell she recognized my fear. Did she also sense my exhilaration? The two did battle in my head almost constantly.

My dreams were not so specific back then. They offered no portent, nor did they show me the man who would be my husband—only his land, which seemed both familiar and strange. The place was very much like Greece: arid, mountainous, and located near the sea. But the contours, dimensions, and feeling of the mountains were different—these were more like hills. I would soon live in this exotic land, surrounded by people who spoke a language unknown to me.

As I'd been unable to sleep, I had been packed for many hours. I'd closed my eyes for a few moments, only to startle awake, heart racing, perspiring heavily. Finally, I gave up, arose, and gathered my things together.

I stepped out onto the balcony barefoot and soundlessly made my way down the stairs. At first, I could just make out the whispering of my guardians but, as I stole closer, I began to make out their words.

"Sabina, dearest, why would you endanger yourself like this?"

My aunt is crying. No, she is sobbing! What is this? I've never known Sabina to shed a tear, even on the day I wounded her deeply with my words.

Barely, I heard the name *Amara.*

My mother. She is talking about my mother!

I felt something give way deep in my chest at the sound of that beloved name.

Amara. Mother.

Then everything went black.

CHAPTER SIX

Sejanus finally spoke. I had not realized it was a contest, but from the look in the Praetorian's eye, Sejanus thought so. His gaze emanated enmity.

"Lucius."

"*Salve*, Sejanus."

He looks the same. How many years has it been...at least fifteen, since those days when we were impossibly young; boys playing at the games of men. But none of it was ever a game for you, Sejanus, and look how far you have come. Head of the Praetorian Guard. Head bodyguard of the Emperor. But it's not enough, is it? Not even this role is sufficient to satisfy your appetite for power, fame, and adulation. Your eyes are wholly devoid of light. Clearly, you hate me still. Or, more likely, you hate everyone who is of no use to you.

As I stood there contemplating his character, I realized how unsurprised I was at the rapid ascension of Sejanus through the ranks. His ambition had been evident even when our cheeks were still smooth. Although his given name was Lucius, like my own, he had discarded it as childish and refused to answer to anything but *Sejanus*. Somehow, he'd persuaded even the coarse instructors to call him by his preferred name, as if *Lucius* had died in childhood. The implication was obvious: Sejanus believed that I, Lucius Pontius Pilate, had preferred to remain a child, answering to the name given me by my mother, while he was a true legionnaire.

Sejanus's sudden renaming had come just at the time of his losses in the chariot races, and I had wondered at the coincidence. Roman legionary training was arduous to be sure, but even those in charge of it had been young once. They understood the psychology of boys eager for manhood—the urgency of their desire to prove themselves worthy of belonging to the world's finest army.

Although Sejanus excelled at most of the training exercises—marathons, gymnastics, marksmanship, and the like—he lost the chariot races handily. And each time to me. The aftermath of our last match was horrific. The instructors had tried to stop the mayhem but did not act in time. Sejanus had gotten so angry at his horses' inability to carry him to victory over my splendid team that he had thrown his javelin into the chest of his lead Arabian, goring him and causing the other three to fall and break their legs. The animals' injuries were so severe that they had to be put out of their misery. Four fine horses dead because of a lost race.

Finally tiring of his wordless exhibition of mastery, Sejanus smiled insolently. It was more of a grimace than a smile, really. "Emperor Tiberius will see you now, Lucius."

Bowing slightly to my new superior, I revealed nothing. Years of practice had taught me perfect self-control. I merely removed my helmet, held it close to my right side, and followed the praetorians stepping smartly into the inner temple of the new Princeps: the "first person" of Rome.

As we marched into the private quarters of Tiberius, Sejanus hissed in my ear, "Prostrate yourself when you get to his throne. This is the god of the world—show him due honor!"

I knew Tiberius would hate the kowtowing—at least the Tiberius I had known in Germania would. But I did as I was bidden.

"Get up, Lucius! For the sake of Jupiter, don't behave like just one more sycophant, please."

Shaking my head, my smile rueful, I apologized to my old comrade. "What would you have me do then, sir?" From my prone position on the stone floor in front of the throne, I could see nothing. I was grateful for the sudden, jarring cold of the stone on my superheated body, and for the few seconds, I'd bought to collect myself. Tiberius's inner chambers contained a glut of brilliant gold-and-bejeweled statues of Roman gods in myriad shapes and sizes. They seemed to cover every centimeter of the spacious room, and so bright was the blinding light of their reflection in the afternoon sun that it threatened to hurt the eyes.

Tiberius, is this you? The one called "the Exile" after you fled to Rhodes to escape your corrupt mother, Livia, and the ruthless Julia she forced you to marry? May the gods save me from such avaricious women! Have all your noble ideals vanished with the laurel crown on your head?

"GET UP, LUCIUS."

The reverberations from his shout shook several pedestal tables severely enough that a few of the precious objects atop them fell to the floor and smashed into tiny pieces. The shards were sure to embed themselves in the bare feet of the slaves who appeared from nowhere to clean up the mess.

"You can leave us now," Tiberius said sharply to the servants. "You too, Sejanus."

"Imperator, I—" Sejanus bowed as he objected, but a snort from Tiberius cut him short. Prudently, he and his seven praetorians backed out of the chambers.

"*Salve*, Lucius. It has been a very long time."

Tiberius looked to me world-weary, even old. His long, thin face was lined, and his eyes, which had always been vital and alive, reflected heartbreak. His broad shoulders slumped, giving him a shrunken look—as if all of the decisions he'd had to make had diminished him. With good reason, I supposed. After all, he'd left a beloved wife when she was pregnant with their son to marry a woman he hated. And then there were the countless men he had led to their deaths. Perhaps he sensed them all blaming him. Mocking him. *For this, you destroyed us? You threw love and family away for some colored glass and gold? Do your treasures comfort you in the middle of the night?*

As if reading my mind, he said, "Lucius, governing Rome is like holding a she-wolf by the ears. Sejanus has been here under three months, and already he is plotting with the Senate against me." At that, he grabbed the laurel crown on his head and smiled as he twirled it around his right forefinger. "Power...it's what we all want. The gods, men, women...I tell you, it is the most potent of all the intoxicating spirits known to man. Once experienced, we seek more and more of it...."

A sudden clap of thunder seemed to sanctify the words of the sovereign ruler of the world. His smile became laughter as he tossed the crown to me. "Lucius, you'll be getting one of these soon. In Judea, where you will be Prelate!"

CHAPTER SEVEN

ROAD TO DELPHI, MACEDONIA
Claudia Procula

I was transfixed by the story Aunt Sabina was telling. For the first time in twelve years, she talked to me easily, with familiarity, with...love. *What was the cause of this sudden concern for my welfare—a concern so seemingly deep that she had implored her husband to make a journey he considered dangerous and maybe foolhardy? And, even more fundamentally, why was Sabina talking about my mother—after years of total silence about her?*

My psyche was a cauldron of unanswered questions mixed with profound gratitude. Upon my collapse outside the *andron*, Uncle Adrian had dropped all resistance to Sabina's pleas. They would accompany me back to Delphi before my voyage to meet my husband-to-be. The trip would take several weeks—possibly longer.

Adrian must have arranged the transfer of his daily responsibility in the agora and at his farm with great haste that morning. A contubernium of Roman legionnaires on horseback appeared about an hour before their convoy left Athens; clearly, they represented the solution to my uncle's misgivings about our traveling alone along the mountainous road to Delphi. Four soldiers would lead the small group of carriages, while the remaining four would ride in back.

I was intrigued, not frightened, by the appearance of the soldiers. The practical effects of Greece's loss of independence to the Roman Empire were far less traumatic than were the turbulent and violent wars among the Greek city-states. In fact, Roman respect and admiration for the philosophy, laws, and culture of Greece were so profound that the Greek language had been adopted by the wealthy and educated Roman leadership. The relationship between the two countries hardly seemed like that of the conqueror and vanquished. As an Athenian, I was well aware of the benefits we enjoyed as citizens of a senatorial province of Rome. I knew that many of the more recently conquered territories in the Orient and Asia required direct Roman leadership and frequent military intervention to quell the rebellion of the citizenry.

But, precisely how did Uncle Adrian manage to secure an escort of Roman legionnaires at such short notice? I had to wonder...but I knew enough to keep this and my many other questions to myself as I sat back against the pile of cushions arranged behind me on the hard seat. I reveled in my relief and rapture at the sound of Sabina's voice, and her evident forgiveness for my verbal mishap of four years earlier.

"What do you want to know?" she asked me, in response to my question about my own mysterious past.

"Everything," I replied. "Every detail. Even just partial memories. All of it—please?"

Sabina offered me a warm and genuine smile, one I had not seen in a very long time. I couldn't help but wonder if she was thinking about my parents at that very moment. But then the weight of her gaze weighed on me oppressively. I feigned surprise at a puzzling sound and glanced around the confined space, but it was merely to escape her scrutiny. When I looked back at my aunt, she still stared at me.

Frowning, I asked, "Is there something wrong? Have I a horrid blemish on my face, Aunt?" *Am I distressingly plain...even ugly?*

"Claudia, nothing of the kind. In fact, I have been think-ing about what an enchanting combination of your mother's fair-skinned and delicate Greek facial features and the thick, lustrous, almost black hair of your Roman centurion father you possess. The distinctive blend of the two of them is almost startling."

She cocked her head to the right and continued to study me. "You have your father's long Roman nose...which makes your face more arresting than beautiful...yet I can see that you will grow into it quite nicely."

I squirmed at this strange emotional shift. My aunt had mostly ignored me for years and now seemed fascinated by me. I had to admit that it was rather pleasing. I found it reassuring to hear that I was not unattractive—especially from someone who seemed to me the quintessence of beauty. With difficulty, I main-tained eye contact.

"But it is your eyes that command attention, Claudia. They are wholly your own. Your eyes change color depending on the quality of the light, your mood, your clothing. Right now, they are warm and almost copper-colored...dancing with excite-ment, I'd say."

I could feel my cheeks start to burn, but if Sabina no-ticed, she was undeterred. "Of course, your usual attitude in-volves intense observation of your surroundings, and in those moments, your eyes look almost black. Revealing nothing at all. This can be more than a little unsettling, even for those of us who know you best." She paused, then—finally—looked down at her lap. "All in all, Claudia, you have become a lovely woman. You are no longer the gangly, awkward girl of just last year, and those dark eyes of yours have no need of kohl to accent them. You seem serene, child. Extremely self-possessed."

Was I? Had serenity become an attribute of mine?

Finally finished with her analysis of my appearance, countenance, and personality, Sabina launched into the story of her own childhood years with my mother and their parents...my grandparents.

The sound of hooves as the three teams of horses pulled the carriages along was metronomic, calming, an acoustic aid to the memories Sabina shared with me. Rolling back the years, she carried me to a time when she and her little sister, Amara—my mother—were small and care-free sprites living on the beaches of Nauplia. The peaceful beachside town had been her beloved home until her marriage to Adrian at sixteen. It had been a paradise, she told me, filled with the simple joys of family. She shared what it was like to belong to a close-knit, loving family—such a stark contrast to my own upbringing.

Sabina sighed, and I could only imagine what sadness mingled with her happy recollections of childhood, of the images of her fisherman father and contented mother. I got the sense that she was trying hard to divert me from my present and future—to give me a fleeting taste of everyday life as it once was, for the duration of our journey.

"Amara and I were water nymphs," she said dreamily. "Father insisted that in reality, we were daughters of Amphitrite." She paused and cast a critical glance at her own hands and arms. Her pale skin was lightly freckled. "Mother was always shouting at us to come in out of the sun, or risk looking like peasants by the time we were thirty!" Glancing at my olive skin, she added, "You have no such worries, my dear. The sun is far kinder to your skin type." Then, scrutinizing me once more, she declared with finality, "Claudia, you are becoming quite lovely."

The erratic, jarring motion of the carriage made it seem almost as if we were riding on horseback. We had climbed out of coastal Athens and now headed northwest along rocky trails to the Parnassus Mountains, where lay the sacred shrine of

Delphi. I wondered if the remains of my mother and her forbidden lover lay among the rocks; if her spirit infused the waters.

CHAPTER EIGHT

TIBERIUS' TEMPLE, ROME
Lucius Pontius Pilate

I felt dazed. My vision swam as I tried to take in what the emperor had just said.

"Well?" Tiberius queried. He stood beside his throne grinning down at me while I, his young protégé, fingered the laurel crown he had impulsively tossed at me. "Lucius, SAY SOMETHING!" The tone of his voice served to summon his slaves once more, although there were no exploded statues to pick up. The four Syrian men who had scurried out from behind voluminous curtains in the rear of the room looked about furtively, then dashed back whence they had come.

The appointment Tiberius had suggested was far loftier than I'd expected. Prelate of Judea was an extraordinary role for a Tribune who had recently turned thirty-two. Judea was the ancient home of that fractious and unruly group of religious zealots known as the Jews. Because the province was so unstable, it was governed personally by the Emperor, rather than the Senate. This meant that as Prelate, I would once again be directly responsible to Tiberius.

At once, I understood the naked hostility Sejanus had shown me earlier. Valerius Gratus had been the Judean Prelate for over ten years and had been close to fifty at the time of his appointment.

Fingering the laurel wreath while scrambling for words, I thought back about the strange foreboding I'd felt earlier while waiting in the atrium. My beloved military career was indeed over, and this governorship—while an extreme honor—would involve a different kind of a battle from any I'd experienced. I'd be required to fight with weapons I'd never wielded, using strategies I was unfamiliar with and had never desired to learn.

I knew a little about my predecessor; far too little, I suspected. But I recalled that in his attempts to bring peace and stability to the various factions within the Jewish people, Gratus had made no fewer than eight appointments to the high priesthood. The latest was a man named Joseph Caiaphas. I could only hope that there had been wisdom in the choice.

The words of Cicero that I had studied as a schoolboy returned to me as I carefully stepped forward to give back the Emperor's crown: "There are, therefore, instances of civic courage that are not inferior to the courage of the soldier. Indeed, civic service calls for even greater energy and devotion."

In Judea, I would become the chief magistrate and head of the judicial system, carrying the laws of Tiberius's empire into a land that boiled and simmered with religious fervor. I swallowed a torrential deluge of misgivings, bowed deeply, and said, "I am at your service, Princeps. I am eager to accept this great honor. Grateful that you consider me worthy."

Thinking the meeting over, I was beginning to back out of the chambers when Tiberius spoke again. "Lucius, you will need a wife out there. It is not seemly for a Roman Prefect to be a single man."

"In just two months, Princeps, I will have a wife."

Surprise evident in his voice, Tiberius replied, "Good

for you Lucius, good for you! What is the name of this fortunate woman?"

"Claudia, Princeps. Her name is Claudia Procula."

CHAPTER NINE

We stopped, and it seemed as if it wasn't just to water the horses. It was too early in the day to set up camp. I leaned out the side of the carriage as far as possible to watch the soldiers remove the wooden, cloth-covered saddles from their horses. One legionnaire was crouched down beside his mount, clearly worried about the animal's leg. Without thinking, I jumped out of the carriage and quickly walked over to him, ignoring Sabina's startled, "Claudia, where are you going?"

I knelt on the rocky ground. "Is he lame?" I asked the soldier in Latin.

The legionnaire was dumbfounded. His mouth worked, but no words came out. I understood; most Greek women did not speak Latin, or, if they did, it was with a terrible accent. Smiling at him in a way that I hoped was flirty and feminine, I said, "I think I can help. May I touch the horse?"

This time the soldier stammered his agreement—just in time, for I had already stood to calm the animal, who looked skittish from either pain or fatigue. His coat was soaked with sweat and his nostrils flared. In as soothing a tone as I could muster, I murmured, "Aren't you a splendid specimen of Andalusian!"

To my ear, Greek would have sounded far more reassuring, but I doubted this legionnaire or his horse spoke Greek. The sound of my words and the laying on of my cool hands calmed him. I could no longer see the whites of his eyes so I dropped back to my knees, fumbling a bit on a few sharp rocks that I feared might cut through the lavender fabric of the *peplos* Sabina had woven for me. Still murmuring nonsense in Latin, I palpated the horse's leg but felt nothing that would cause lameness. When I lifted its hoof, I found the culprit: Wedged into the right bar—the turning point of the back of the hoof—was a thorn.

By this time, the soldier had knelt beside me, and he saw the problem as well. "*Optime puella*," he said, and grasped the hoof with one hand, intending to pull the thorn out with the other.

"Careful—don't break it off," I cautioned, recalling the problem my uncle had had when one of his slaves had removed only part of a sharp twig from one of his prize horse's hooves. The ensuing infection had festered for over a month.

Nodding, the legionnaire let go of the horse and stood. Rummaging through a leather pack draped over his saddle, he pulled out a sort of grasping tool. By the time he knelt again at my side, a substantial crowd had assembled to watch the operation, which was successful.

I could feel Uncle Adrian's strong arms enfold me. He pulled me to my feet, laughed, then kissed the tip of my nose and gave me a quick hug. "Good work, Caritas," he said. "All of those hours you spent working with my Alessandro and our horses have been put to good use!"

I could see Sabina standing behind her husband, and I hurried to her side to apologize for my hasty gesture. To my surprise, she was smiling even more broadly than Uncle Adrian had. Noting that she held our small bags in her hands, I asked if we were staying where we were.

"Indeed we are!" she said and made a sweeping gesture

that took in all that I had not noticed in my singular focus on the horse. The establishment in front of which we'd stopped was huge—a *stathmos* where all of us, horses and humans, could surely find shelter and food. The barns must have been filled to overflowing with barley. Now I could see my equine friend's nostrils flaring for a different reason. He smelled food.

So this was Thebes, the city leveled by Alexander several centuries earlier. My mind reeled with the myths. This was said to be the birthplace of Hercules, and the site where the Sphinx had posed her famous riddle to Oedipus: "What is a creature that may have two, three, or four feet, can move in air, water, and on land, and moves more slowly the more feet it has?" His correct answer that it was a man had so enraged the Sphinx that she'd leapt to her death from the Theban Acropolis—or so went the myth.

Everywhere I looked, I imagined the glory of the place as it had once been. This was a virtual feast for the imagination of a young girl who had scarcely left her home in Athens. I could spy the ruins of the Cadmean Fortress over a rise beyond the *stathmos* and could not help but consider all the successful battles fought by the city-state against Athens and Sparta. And then came the final and devastating destruction, brought upon the city by its own rebellion against the peaceful union of Greek city-states that Philip of Macedonia had instituted. *The hubris of man continually foments his passion and lust for power.*

My stomach growled so loudly that both Sabina and Adrian laughed. "Come," said my uncle. "Let's go wash and then enjoy some wine and good food."

CHAPTER TEN

"Well, Quintillus, we've made far better time than I had planned. After just three days, we are on the outskirts of Aquileia. At this rate, we may even reach Caesarea before the end of the month. What do you think, Quintillus? Can we make it before the Fides?"

As it was already the middle of September, getting to Judea by the first of October would be a remarkable feat. I smiled at the thought; Fides was one of my favorites on the long list of Roman gods and goddesses. Although I thought of them as mythical, this goddess stood for the virtues of trust and good faith I worked hard to personify.

The centurion's gaze remained on me for mere seconds before he returned to surveying the Aquileian landscape—on guard, tirelessly. Although we traveled within the confines of the Empire, Quintillus was well aware of the temptations presented by a phalanx of Roman soldiers to young and foolish boys native to the land. Our preference was to disarm them peacefully, or simply scare them off with warnings, but if they surprised our legionnaires, they risked their own deaths. The day before, in

Bononia, a ragtag group of four Etruscans—none older than thirteen or fourteen—had appeared out of nowhere, brandishing swords and hollering. They'd been cut down in minutes. No one celebrated their deaths.

Quintillus and I had been together since that long-ago battle after which I had become Tribune. That had been just eight years ago, but on days like this one, it felt like twenty. It had been eight non-stop years of death—luckily, not our own.

At least three times throughout those years, I'd felt certain my time had come. On the ground under a substantial Germanian warrior; alone and cornered by three horsemen; and finally, standing and waiting for a mortal blow I was sure would come. Each time, Quintillus had appeared out of nowhere, brandishing his glaudius or pila, or—in that last case—one in each hand. Two of the four Germanians confronting me had toppled, my comrade's swords finding their hearts. The other two ran.

Quintillus's skill on the battlefield exceeded that of any man I had ever known or studied. Tiberius had pinned five medals on his chest, Augustus, three—all before he'd turned twenty. Frequently, I wondered just what I had done to merit the allegiance and steadfastness of this centurion.

Like me, Quintillus was a Samnite. Proud, stalwart, and fearsome warriors, the Samnites lived along the ridge of the Apennine Mountains in south-central Italy. They'd come very close to defeating the Romans in three different wars, but ultimately, the Romans had always won the day. Practically speaking, their country was no more.

A man of few words, when Quintillus chose to speak, I listened carefully and usually took his advice. That included his counsel regarding this achingly long, 5,000-mile journey. Tiberius had sent a wax tablet by messenger, offering to pay for eight of us to make the trip to Caesarea by sea. I was sorely tempted, knowing that it would cut some three weeks off the trip, but something had pricked at the back of my mind, telling me to *be careful*.

Scrutinizing the tablet, I noticed that it lacked the seal of Tiberius Caesar. I took it to the stables, where Quintillus was working with the horses, to ask for his opinion. He looked up from the stallion he was grooming, expressionless.

"We could go by sea—saving us many days," I said. "Doing so would allow me to accompany Claudia from Athens to Caesarea. What are your thoughts, my friend?"

He studied me. Although Quintillus was aware of my impending marriage, he had never mentioned it or asked me any questions about my wife-to-be. Not that it would have mattered if he had; I knew next to nothing about Claudia Procula. I wondered if he would say something about her now, but his gaze dropped to study the tablet for a moment. Then he raised an eyebrow and derisively muttered, "Sejanus."

There wasn't a legionnaire who did not know Sejanus, but Quintillus had been a trainer when Sejanus and I were just beginning our service. He had witnessed the brutality of the young man in the wake of our last chariot race. A soldier's horse was his partner; its well-being could make the difference between life and death for the legion. Quintillus had viewed Sejanus's selfish, wholly unwarranted savagery as iniquity, not merely a character flaw. In the trainer's mind, the young legionnaire's actions had warranted far worse than the flogging and two weeks of double drills that he had suffered. Quintillus would have executed the young soldier, nothing less, and considered the act virtuous.

Each January fifth, when Quintillus recited the Sacramentum Militare, he did so with heartfelt conviction: "I shall faithfully execute all that the Emperor commands, I shall never desert the service, and I shall not seek to avoid death for the Roman Republic." His grandfather had been one of the first Roman legionnaires under the Marian reforms instituted by Gaius Marius, and none who knew him or fought with him ever doubted that he would gladly die for the Empire.

In the beginning, the army of the Roman Republic had been comprised of citizen-soldiers. Only men of wealth and property could join the military, as they alone could afford the cost of their own arms and equipment. But with the drop of new citizens volunteering, Marius began to recruit all able-bodied men, even the landless poor, promising them weapons and equipment from Rome. Effectively, he had broken the law, but his initiative ended up saving the city from attack by Germanian tribes. His reforms were eventually made law, and resulted in a paid standing army equipped to handle the expanding Roman Empire.

The idea of marshaling an eight-man unit to accompany me to Judea had been Sejanus's. As Prefect of the Praetorian Guards, he had the authority to make it happen. Once Quintillus had spoken his name, I could picture Sejanus writing out the spurious message and sending his slave to deliver it. His face must have exhibited the same loathing I'd been subjected to during our last meeting at the palace. He'd thought he was dangling a temptation that could not be refused—one that would end with the humiliation of his arch enemy.

Quintillus said no more about Sejanus, nor did he take any time to ponder the offer. He merely reminded me of the momentousness of the first impression I would make upon my arrival. It was critical that the new Judean Prelate look like he had the full power of the Roman Empire behind him. Eight of us traveling alone, arriving by sea, would look weak and insubstantial, maybe even timid. This was precisely the impression that Sejanus had hoped I'd make on the canny zealots of Judea.

CHAPTER ELEVEN

THEBES, MACEDONIA
Claudia Procula

"Would you like a bit of wine with your dinner, young lady?"

Looking across the table at my aunt and uncle, I blushed with delight when Sabina answered for me in the affirmative. I had never had wine before. Sabina and Adrian did not drink it with dinner at home; the only time I'd ever seen it in the house was in the *andron,* when Adrian was entertaining his friends and business associates.

The serving woman was back in a flash with a large jug filled to the brim with red wine. Pouring a healthy amount into each of our goblets, she smiled and said, "Your dinner will be ready in just a few minutes."

As she raised her cup to Adrian and me, Sabina's smile was broader than I had ever seen it, her mood light, festive, and gay. I thought I understood why.

"Claudia, may the gods shine on you," she said, "but most especially, *your* God—the One who reigns over all the rest."

Both Adrian and I drank deeply, each of us recalling the time Sabina and I had spoken about gods and God.

She laughed gracefully. "I'll admit that it's humiliating to be taught about God by your ten-year-old niece, but..." She paused, abruptly solemn, and glanced over at Adrian. He nodded almost imperceptibly—but I caught it.

They have talked about that day. More than once!

"I was angry at you, Claudia. For years. Unjustly." With her cheeks flushed from the wine and emotion and those expressive eyes glistening in the light of the candlelight, my aunt was so beautiful that she took my breath away.

"You see," she continued, "you said the exact words that your mother had. Before she left for Delphi. Word for word."

I should have been surprised by this revelation, but I wasn't. Maybe it was because we were approaching Delphi, or because I was now a woman. The dreams had begun again, and with them came a sharpening of my vision—not the literal kind, but another level of perception that had nothing to do with my eyesight. I knew things that I'd never been taught. My tending to the horse earlier that day was but one example. Yes, I had been around Uncle Adrian's stable throughout my childhood, but no one had ever shown me the hoof of a horse. Yet, I knew there might be a thorn, and exactly where to look for it. What's more, I had absolutely no fear of that frightened ton of flesh looking at me fearfully, the whites of his eyes rolling. It was almost as if I could read his thoughts and he mine.

I had developed a confidence far beyond what I'd felt upon mastering scholarly readings. Instead of just knowledge—or maybe in addition to it—I felt I was in possession of a sense of kindness, a generosity of spirit far beyond what was normal for a fifteen-year-old soul. I was readying myself for an apprenticeship in this new kind of wisdom that I could not properly express in language.

I sat in silence, vicariously enjoying Sabina's delight in being with the man she loved. Instead of her usual light dinner with her friends, she sat dining with her husband. And, as if that were not enough, she now understood some things about herself and her baby sister—my mother. Things that had been long suppressed. Sabina's joy was contagious; it seemed to spill out and over the whole of the large dining room—the *gleumata*—and imprint itself onto the faces of other diners.

I had read about these places designed specifically for drinking and revelry. Most of the long wooden tables were filled with men and a few women—on their way to intoxication, from the sounds of their conversations, which were loud enough to be easily overheard. I noticed one dinner table, far across the room, occupied by what seemed to be a family traveling just like us. Elsewhere, three women approached a table of soldiers, hesitated for a few moments, then took seats next to the legionnaires. As I watched, one of the women stood up, giggling and weaving from side to side, and extended her hand to the man she'd sat next to. Hand in hand, they left through one of the exit doors.

I was spellbound, knowing exactly where they were headed and what they would be doing.

"Claudia..." Adrian could not hide his amusement at my fascination with the ways of men and women fueled by wine. Suppressing his smile with difficulty, he looked up at the serving girl, who was standing by me looking anxious—as if she'd done something wrong. Apparently, she had asked me more than once if I wanted fish or chicken, but I'd been oblivious to her queries. Hastily, I replied, "Oh—the fish, please. I am sorry I didn't hear you before...I suppose I was woolgathering."

The girl nodded but did not return my smile. I doubted she had a lot to smile at. Very dark complected and about my age, I guessed that she was a slave from Syria or Thrace. I wondered if her duties extended beyond serving meals, and suspected they did.

When I turned my attention back to Sabina, she was leaning over to kiss Adrian's cheek. This was a surprisingly public demonstration of affection, and I was touched by the tenderness with which my uncle regarded her.

Why did they never have children? They are obviously in love, even after so many years...

Sabina's next comment took me aback. Had I inadvertently spoken my thoughts aloud, or had her tongue simply been loosened by the wine she was unaccustomed to?

"I had an accident when I was a couple of years younger than you, Claudia," she said quietly. "One that left me infertile." As I watched her, the joy drained from her face. "Amara, who was just five years old when it happened, stood at the foot of my bed and declared that one day, she would have a baby. A girl. And that child would end up becoming my daughter."

Now, the tears coursed freely down her face, taking with them the carefully applied kohl and ochre. Ignoring the effect, Sabina pushed on. "I am so very sorry, Claudia. You were such a tiny little thing. But each time I looked at you, all I could think of was my baby sister, those astounding words. How could she have known?"

I am sure that the abrupt silence in that room filled with intoxicated people existed only in my mind. And yet, it seemed that everything came to a halt.

CHAPTER TWELVE

PERGAMUM, ASIA MINOR
Lucius Pontius Pilate

After over two weeks of driving the horses and our eight-hundred men ten hours a day, we reached the outskirts of Pergamum, capital of the empire's province of Asia.

I had never been this far east and was surprised and impressed by the condition of the roads we had built throughout the empire. Although I knew that our soldiers had begun working with surveyors on them almost immediately upon gaining new territories, I'd not seen the evidence in far-flung places such as Asia. My heart swelled with pride at the engineering marvel of these roads, which eased our eastward journey considerably. If these conditions held as we continued, I calculated that Caesarea was just ten or eleven days away.

We decided that a celebration of our good fortune was in order. Cheers resounded throughout the beautiful land about ten miles south of the city when I announced that we would rest where we stood for the next three days. Our temporary camp was on the bank near the mouth of a large river. Thankfully, we had seen no more rebellious youngsters since Bononia. The towering trees offered excellent protection from an ambush, which seemed unlikely since our survey of the area revealed only birds above and many fish leaping from the waters of the clear river. We would eat well that evening.

The soldiers were divided into contuberniums, sub-units of eight, to quickly construct the vast camp. The first unit paced out the rectangular dimensions to begin digging the *fossae.* A one-by-one-and-a-half meter trench surrounded the entire camp and would serve as a defensive trap in case of a surprise attack.

Servants led pack mules carrying tent poles, folder tents, and heavy equipment, and the contubernium tents went up quickly. These large, eight-man structures encircled the perimeter. Each Centurion and Tribune had his own tent and the largest—mine—was in the center.
Within two hours, the encampment was complete.

Quintillus and I sat sipping wine in my tent. I suspected many of the men were on their way into the city in search of a bathhouse, followed by a *popina* where they could enjoy wine and women.

Quintillus broke the silence. "Claudia is the niece of Adrian—the Greek at the last chariot race at Circus Maximus." It was a statement, not a question. Neither of us had mentioned her name for over two weeks, but the man spoke as if he were replying to something I had said just a moment earlier.

I smiled. It had always been that way between the two of us. "Yes, she is," I responded.

"He is a wealthy man." Another question masquerading as a statement.

I smiled again, enjoying the pure pleasure of sitting motionless on a cushion instead of a bouncing atop a horse. I thought back to that day at Circus Maximus and the strange confluence of circumstances that had placed me in the company of a wealthy landowner from Athens. "A man with a future written in the stars needs a wife," he'd said. "An extraordinary woman." The Greek was commanding, eloquent, and persuasive. "Her name is Claudia. She is my ten-year-old niece, daughter of a Roman centurion. In five years, she will be ready to wed. Claudia speaks fluent Latin as well as Greek and has just mastered the ideas within my own copy of Plato's *Republic*. Her education will continue under my tutelage. Your bride will be thoroughly schooled in moral education and *ludus litterarius*, as well as philosophy."

The Greek's knowledge of and adherence to the basics of classical Roman education did not escape his listener.

"Her dowry will be extravagant, as my wife and I have no children of our own."

Adrian seemed an honest man. The omission of the identity of the girl's mother must have seemed advisable for some reason, and I didn't press him. He pulled out a scroll and handed it to me.

Unfurling it, I saw that it was headed, *Pledge of Betrothal*, and read on:

> *Claudia Procula, the niece of Adrian and Sabina Procula, is betrothed to Lucius Pontius Pilate upon the occasion of her fifteenth birthday, September 5, Julian Year 28. Her dowry includes 1000 drachmas, a Gallic slave, and 1200 minae for the wedding celebration, set to begin on Saturnalia of that year.*

I was mesmerized by this Greek. He reminded me of a tutor my father had hired for me as a boy, the man who introduced me to Cincinnatus, Cicero, and some of the Greek philosophers.

Claudia. I had never heard the name. Pronouncing it again in my mind, I decided I liked the sound of it. As Adrian Procula and I shook hands, I could see Quintillus standing behind the Greek. Expression inscrutable.

That was five years ago. I was beginning to sense how quickly time passed. Adrian had prescribed our wedding day as the beginning of Saturnalia: I would be married to Claudia Procula by the start of the new year. Just as every Roman did, I observed the joy of that feast. The gifts, festivities, and lightheartedness made this a most opportune day for a wedding.

That said, my religious beliefs tended more toward ritual than faith. My father, a farmer, had taught me the prayer to Father Mars, and from the time I was a small boy, we would make the *adortio* upon entering our home altar. On each of the four March Festival Days, we carefully prepared the offering—the *suovetauilla*: a triple sacrifice of pig, bull, and ram.

As I entered into my adult life as a legionnaire, that ritual remained unchanged. The first meals the cooks made upon completion of the fort and temple outside of Pergamum consisted of the fruits of the triple sacrifice. As Prelate and former Legate, I was first to enter the temple *capite velato* at our camp. A fold of my toga covering my head. I raised my right hand to my lips and rotated my body to the right, as prescribed, and intoned:

> *Father Mars, I pray and beseech thee that thou*
> *be gracious and merciful to me, my house, and*
> *my household; to which intent I have bidden*
> *this suovetaurilia to be led around my land, my*
> *ground, my farm; that thou keep away, ward off*
> *and remove sickness, seen and unseen, barren-*
> *ness and destruction, ruin and unseasonable in-*
> *fluence; and that thou permit my harvests, my*
> *grain, my vineyards and my plantations to flour-*
> *ish and come to good issue, preserve in health*
> *my shepherds and my flocks, and give good*
> *health and strength to me, my house,and my*
> *household To this intent, to the intent of purify-*
> *ing my farm, my land, and my ground, and of*
> *making an expiation, as I have said, deign to ac-*
> *cept the offering of these suckling victims. Fa-*
> *ther Mars, to the same intent, deign to accept*
> *these suckling offerings.*

I thought back to that day five years earlier, when I'd heard, "Tribune, where are you going? Caesar has bid you appear at the palace to receive the laurel wreath."

We had been returning from that first Germania war. My appearance at the Circus had been a spontaneous, perhaps even frivolous move on my part.

A brand-new Tribune, just twenty-eight years of age, full of myself and reckless, I'd decided to stop and indulge in one last chariot race. I suspected—correctly, as it would turn out—that it would be my last. Although more exhausted than I had ever been, I *needed* to experience the thrill of this other kind of battle.

Quintillus had followed me—unhappily—into the arena.

I had forgotten the immensity of the place. More than 250,000 people filled the stadium. A full purple awning covered more than thirty rows. *Was Caesar Augustus here? Would he be watching me compete recklessly against charioteers who raced several times per week when I myself had not stepped into a chariot for six years?*

The colors worn by the charioteers were a rainbow signifying their native countries; blues and pale yellow, with the red and gold of the Romans, predominating. How was it that I felt impelled to enter a race that I had not even known about, starting in under a quarter of an hour? How was it that the team hastily commandeered for me consisted of friendly horses from my days of legionary training? They snickered and snorted happily when I approached, prompting their usurped driver to give them—and me—a look of disgust as he wandered off unsteadily.

Was he drunk? What if I hadn't appeared?

I flashed back to that dreadful day when Sejanus had killed his horses in anger over his loss to me. These horses had nothing to fear, and they knew it as I whispered into each one's ear. The lead horse, Ademus, snuffled back.

They remember me!

There was very little time before the start of the race, so I beckoned to Quintillus to jog up to the herald's booth and enter my name into the competition so we could be announced. Seconds after he returned, the Emperor stood and dropped the cloth, signaling that it was time to get into position for the start of the race. I had just enough time to stare pointedly at Quintillus as we lined up at the gate.

Waiting for us at the palace? Quintillus had the grace to smile and nod at the fact that Caesar may have "bid me appear at the palace," but that we would have been waiting there for quite some time, as he was here.

I could see the bloodstained whites of the eyes of the charioteer to my right. No more than five feet separated us. He was in gold—a Corinthian. His team was three big chestnuts and a Persian, taller and stockier than my Arabs. *Would their size be an advantage?* On my left was a diminutive Macedonian I estimated to be half my size and weight. *Undoubtedly, his lightness will augment his agility and speed.*

Before my self-doubts could paralyze me, the trumpets sounded, the gates opened, and we were off.

The noise! How do these animals stand the constant bedlam?

Strangely, by the end of the first lap, it had all come back to me. Ademus and his fellow horses were fast, but they knew seven laps was a long race. I could see the Corinthian advancing on my right—too fast, too early. He was driving recklessly. I pulled back on my reins; getting stuck between a foolish driver and the wall of the track could mean death. My boys responded instantly.

By the fifth lap, only five of thirty-five teams remained in the race. One by one, all of the other teams had lost wheels or crashed. Three charioteers—one of them the Corinthian—had collided and been dragged a few feet, but all three had managed to sever the reins from around their waists and escape the deadly hooves overtaking them.

During the sixth lap, I began to let the reins loose, then looser. Ademus lowered his head, raised it, and then all four ran like the wind.

How was it that someone began to chant my name? It must have been someone who had witnessed the dreadful battle just days earlier. Soon, the entire crowd was on its feet shouting *Lucius! Pontius! Pilate!*

Quintillus, reading my mind, as usual, interrupted my recollections.

"Five years, Lucius. They have vanished." Shaking his head, he chuckled. "I used to laugh at my father when he spoke about how quickly the years pass by." He was mirroring my own thoughts as we both pondered the passage of time since that fortuitous meeting with the Greek. He poured another generous serving of wine, first into my cup, then into his, and raised his arm in a toast.

"To the man with his future written in the stars."

We drank long into that quiet night, listening to the pleasant gurgle of the river. Later, we heard the sounds of men returning from the city, all appetites sated. Finally, we slept—all but the two soldiers on watch.

CHAPTER THIRTEEN

My smile was broad as I opened my mouth to reply to Sabina with the expected, *Of course, I forgive you, Aunt. You have nothing in the world to be sorry for.* Part of me was astonished at the foreknowledge my five-year-old mother had demonstrated—but only part. I recognized that small child and wondered at our connection.

But the words of absolution refused to leave my lips. All of a sudden, I felt nailed to the chair I sat on, overwhelmed with foreboding about my life and the man I would marry. A deep and profound sorrow threatened to consume me.

Just then, the serving girl materialized at our table with an overflowing tray of food. Carefully placing platters of lamb in front of Sabina and Adrian and a succulent-looking fish dish in front of me, the server pulled a variety of condiments from her many-pocketed apron and placed them before us, then stood back to ask, "Do you need anything else?"

"No, thank you, this looks excellent," said my uncle, inhaling audibly. We had not eaten since the night before and then only some cheese and olives. Sensing our impatience to begin, the server managed a tentative smile and floated away.

The aroma and appearance of the plates excited my appetite and drove away the awful presentiment that had threatened to overwhelm me. Glancing over at my aunt and uncle, I could see they shared my eagerness. Without another word, we began to eat.

After a half hour when my only thoughts were of what lay on the plate before me, I sat back, satiated, and gazed at Sabina. She was absorbed in cutting the last bit of lamb off the bone and did not meet my gaze until she'd popped the morsel into her mouth.

"What?" she said, staring back at me with her hand over her mouth like a child caught eating a forbidden dessert. She looked ten years younger without the makeup that had been washed away by her tears.

"Aunt Sabina, you asked if I could forgive you, and I've yet to answer." I extended my arms as if to embrace the room, and continued, "What's to forgive?" Before she could regain her earlier mordant mood or infer that I was trivializing her concern, I hastily continued, "I think I understand how painful my presence must have been in those early days. Each time you looked at me or heard my voice, you must have been reminded of your sister's dire prediction. There is no need to forgive a natural human response to grief."

I caught the glance that passed between my aunt and uncle and knew what they were thinking. *She is just like Amara. She has her gifts. Perhaps even greater ones.*

It was as if they'd spoken these thoughts aloud, but I didn't dwell on them, for fear our unaccustomed lightness would come to an end. Taking another sip of the wine, I leaned forward across the table. "Tell me about him," I said—but perhaps my change of subject was too abrupt. Sabina lifted an eyebrow in puzzlement and Adrian remained silent.

I clarified. "Tell me about the man you would have me

marry in six weeks time."

Once again, a glance passed between my guardians—this time prolonged.

I waited.

Uncle Adrian opened his mouth, then closed it. He stared down at his empty plate and cleared his throat. Finally, he met my gaze. "Claudia, until this moment you have resisted our attempts to tell you about him. Why now?"

Sabina busied herself by toying with the remains of her dinner.

"Uncle, I feel...light. The wine is very likely a factor in that, but more than that, I feel such immense gratitude for you and Aunt Sabina. I am aware of the sacrifices my presence in your lives has required...." I hesitated, then continued. "I am so grateful for your love. I feel...*happy*." As I watched their faces grow tender, I wondered at the truth of that simple statement, and at the sense of peace, I felt deep down for the first time I could remember. I was learning an all-important lesson: this life is filled with confusion, sorrow, pain, and disappointment. When moments of untrammeled joy such as this one come along, one must hold on to them—make them last.

I knew I would treasure this moment for the rest of my life. I couldn't help wondering if my mother was, in some mystical way, guiding me. "Uncle, for the first time, I feel ready to begin my new life. Before, back in Athens, all I felt was reluctance...to leave the life of a child and learn the ways of a woman. Now, I find myself excited, fearful, and curious, all at once." I stared at him and Sabina, willing them to understand.

Adrian glanced at his wife, then turned back to regard me gravely. "Right after your tenth birthday, Claudia...do you recall that I traveled to Rome on business?"

At my answering nod, his eyes glowed, and he grew animated. "As a member of our Agora, I had been invited to a meeting to discuss the expansion of the Pax Romana with Caesar

Augustus, but the Emperor was still very ill. There were several of us from the provinces who had traveled for many days to make the meeting. Marcus Calvus was the consul charged with organizing the conference. He and ten other Senators opened their homes to those of us who had traveled long distances."

Turning to Sabina, he took her hand and said, "I wish you had been there, my love. You would have enjoyed meeting Marcus's wife, Felicia."

Sabina squeezed his hand, then murmured, "Do go on, Adrian. I've not heard all of these details before."

"A friend of Marcus's invited us all to the chariot races at Circus Maximus. Apparently, the man had some of his own chariot teams entered." Adrian's broad grin at the memory took twenty years off of his face. "I always wanted to enter the chariot races myself, but..." His voice trailed off, and a faraway look passed over him.

"You were too busy with the farm," I interjected, "along with your responsibilities in the Agora and...life!" Both Sabina and Adrian chuckled at my completion of his thought.

"Ah, but these races...They were *larger* than life, my dear! Neither of you can imagine the number of people at the stadium that day—why I'll wager there were 250,000! That is the equivalent of the whole population of Athens!"

Both Sabina and I exclaimed aloud. It truly was unimaginable.

"Marcus tried to explain to me the significance of a last-minute switch in charioteers, but the noise of the people cheering made it impossible to hear anything. He signaled that he would explain later. The stadium had staggered gates that were spring-loaded. You would not believe the veritable explosion when thirty-five four-horse chariots burst forth and thundered through seven laps. What a contest!"

Both Sabina and I had our elbows on the table at this point, listening intently. I had never heard my uncle so passionate about anything—not even Plato.

"With perfect timing, the man who had entered the race at the very last minute made his move. Deftly, he edged past the other teams one by one, somehow—miraculously—avoiding the crashed chariots of those who had miscalculated. My host and I were on our feet cheering, along with the rest of the crowd, at this brave man's audacity and command of his horses. I had never seen or heard such an uproar."

Adrian's eyes shone as he brought his story to its breathless conclusion. "Suddenly, the brave charioteer crossed the finish—he had won. First, a few voices, then many, then all cheered his name: *Lucius Pontius Pilate*. When I turned a questioning eye to my host, he explained that this brave man had arrived directly from battle in Germania, where he had been instrumental in an important win. For his efforts, he had been elevated by Tiberius to the rank of Tribune at just twenty-eight years of age. I could hear the murmur as the crowd talked about his exploits just as we were."

At this point, my uncle turned and looked directly into my eyes. "I decided then and there, my dear, that *this* man was your destiny."

CHAPTER FOURTEEN

Lucius Pontius Pilate

Finally, we arrived in Caesarea, capital of Judea. With a population of around 400,000, it was about the same size as Athens and
two thirds the size of Rome.

*An entire town constituted of dazzling white stone...the
reports of it do not do it justice. How would one put words to a
place such as this?*

I had to close my eyes against the glare of this brilliant
sea of white. The harbor alone was more magnificent than any
I'd seen. Without being sure why, I led the cohort—800 Roman
cavalry officers including the subalterns—along the promenade
of the most famous harbor in the world, rather than directly north
to the palace: my new home.

Recalling Sejanus's attempt to taint my entrance into
Judea, I slowed my stallion to a walk, fully aware of the majestic
impression made by the horses in perfect cadence and the bright
scarlet-and-gold uniforms contrasting with the stark white stone.
Truly, our overall aspect was nothing short of magnificent.

Quintillus pulled his horse up to ride beside me for just
a moment. When he was sure he'd gotten my attention, he bowed

his head, then lifted it again to meet my gaze. His eyes were luminous. Pride, respect, and admiration—*This was the perfect way for the new Prelate to arrive.*

Then he pulled his horse to a complete stop to permit the long line of soldiers astride their horses to advance ahead. The centurion would be the last in the procession.

The men understood their roles, and, despite having put in ten-to-twelve-hour days during the past week, sat taller in their saddles. The slow rhythm of the horses was a welcome relief after the canter that had gotten them here. Even the horses perked up as more and more people flooded the streets and rooftops, attracted by the sound of our entrance into the walled city. Although it was October and not yet midday, the intense desert heat rose in shimmery waves off of the broad roads.

From astride our horses, my men and I surveyed the beauty of the place and marveled at its Roman engineering. We could see the aqueduct bringing water from many miles away, the stadium, Caesar's temple…and finally, the Hippodrome, where the chariot races were held. Wistfully, I gazed at the immense circular stone structure. *It looks as large as the Circus Maximus in Rome!* I thought as I recalled that Herod had been granted the title of King of Judea by the Roman Senate in acknowledgment of his genius in creating Caesarea, as well as his unflagging loyalty. The small naval station at Straton's Tower had been a dilapidated Jewish settlement until Herod had seen past the unforgiving coastline to envision and then execute the first man-made harbor in the world. My heart swelled with pride at the symmetry, style, and utility of this marvelous, ingenious fortification.

Roman engineers had brilliantly executed Herod's sagacious vision by sinking numerous large wooden frames filled with stones and rubble deep under the water, along with Roman hydraulic concrete. The concrete, made by combining volcanic ash, lime, and water, hardened into fifty-ton rocks, effectively creating an underwater foundation for a breakwater that would extend more than 1,500 feet into the ocean in a horseshoe shape, thus protecting the entire bay. Massive white columns had then been erected on the promenade to form the mainstay of the wall that encircled the city.

As I led the cohort slowly along the promenade, I noted inlets in the wall that provided landing places for mariners and a circular terrace for disembarking passengers. Adjacent to the harbor were rows of houses, also built of white stone on streets radiating symmetrically from the promenade.

Where there had been just a few people—maybe fifty—, there were now a few hundred, and more were assembling by the moment as our convoy passed through the city.

Well Herod, after seeing the marvels of your city, I am eager to experience the wonders of the palace you built. I am confident it will not disappoint!

Without thinking, I stopped and dismounted to stare up at the colossal statues at the mouth of the harbor. I had to tip my head back to salute the image of Augustus Caesar, a fifty-foot-statue cleverly conjoined with one of the twenty-, maybe thirty-foot columns as if it sat on a gigantic pedestal. Just as I did so, the murmuring of the now several hundred people gathered faded to silence.

As one, they turned toward a group of men hurrying down the main street.

The lead figure was dressed exotically, a large turban with a vertical blue stripe covering most of his white hair. The hem of his white linen tunic flapped in time with his rapid strides. Over it, he wore a blue robe; an apron-like garment was tied over that, featuring gold writing in what looked to me like Hebrew.

Caiaphas. It has to be.

My men remained mounted, the strain in their postures becoming evident as a few of the stallions began to snake—lowering and waving their heads side to side.

It would take only a word, a gesture, from one of these Judeans to incite mayhem. I wondered if the men held rocks in the pockets of those capacious robes. The crowd's silence was ominous as if waiting for an invitation to aggression. I had to do something. Immediately.

Jumping up onto the base of one of the columns supporting the statue of Caesar Augustus, I shouted in Greek to my men, "Welcome to our new home! Thank you all for your steadfastness during this month-long journey. Quintillus will lead you to your new quarters so that you can water and rest your horses and get some rest yourselves. The first few glasses of wine are on me!"

I knew that most of my soldiers did not speak Greek but would get the gist of my words instantly: *We are released!* An appreciative roar arose from the men as they took off. Even the apprehensive townspeople broke into smiles at their exuberance.

I suspected that these priests spoke even better Greek than I, and knew precisely what I had just done. Perhaps they wondered if their new Prelate was a fool to leave himself wholly unprotected.

CHAPTER FIFTEEN

CAESAREA, JUDEA
Lucius Pontius Pilate

While waiting for the priest and his entourage to approach, I recalled Cicero's description of the Jews as people born to be slaves. The immensity of my new responsibility weighed as heavily on me as if it were one of the gigantic stone pillars on the promenade.

I ran through my mission in my head. *I am the personal representative of Tiberius to these fractious groups of religious zealots who fight among themselves over each jot of their strange, endless lists of laws. Because of the instability of this place, Judea remains under the Emperor instead of the Senate. Each and every rule and code that is passed by Rome is up to me to enforce. Especially the tax code.*

Although my position was now higher than Legate, the head of a Legion of 5000, I had decided to wear the uniform of a tribune for my last journey as a soldier. Hot and uncomfortable as the helmet, shoulder plates, woolen tunic, body armor, and shield were, I was proud to wear the scarlet-and-gold symbol of the empire I would happily have given my life for.

Roman, remember by your strength to rule

Earth's peoples—for your arts are to be these:
To pacify, to impose the rule of law,
to spare the conquered, battle down the proud.

More and more people had amassed in the five minutes that I'd waited, and now there were hundreds of them and just one of me. I realized that my decision to stand at the foot of a statue that the Jews considered blasphemous might have been imprudent. I considered but quickly dismissed the idea of moving. If I changed position now, it could be interpreted as weakness.

As I shifted my weight from my left leg to my right, I mused about the ease with which I could be killed. A few words from just one of these strange people and a mob could be incited. I had seen it happen before: a large group of civilians milling about, no weapons in evidence, seemingly peaceful when suddenly a young boy decides to be a patriot. Within minutes, the friendly crowd turns into a murderous mob.

Quintillus knew the danger I was in when I sent him away with the men. I could tell from the look on his face. It was the same on the day we went into Circus Maximus instead of up to Caesar Augustus's palace. 'Don't be a fool, Lucius,' his glance had told me. And yet, there was admiration there, too.

Are my actions fatuous or courageous? This question will be answered in just a few minutes. The time it takes to distinguish the valiant from the craven can be just seconds...

During my formative education, I had been fairly single-minded. I'd wanted to be a soldier. But then my favorite Greek tutor had introduced me to philosophy—to his beloved Stoicism.

To wealthy Roman families, the *Grammaticus* could be taught well by Romans, but a good education presumed a foundation in philosophy—and that required a Greek tutor. Demetrius had been my favorite. Patient, skilled, and most importantly, a lover of learning, Demetrius had known precisely how to win the heart and mind of a twelve-year-old Roman boy: immersion in the battle of Thermopylae and the feats of the Spartan commander, Dienekes. In this chapter of history, 300 Spartans held off a Persian army of close to a million men.

As I watched the crowd around me grow larger and more restless, I could hear Demetrius quoting a soldier imploring Dienekes: "The Persian soldiers are so numerous that when they fire, the mass of their arrows blocks out the sun."

Laughing, Dienekes had replied, "Good! Then we'll have our battle in the shade."

At the approach of the Jewish religious leaders, I sprang off the column and pulled myself to my full height. I did not consider myself a tall man, but next to these Jews, I felt gigantic.

We make a most colorful pair, Caiaphas and I. I wonder if he is sweating as profusely as I under those three layers of cloth?

Striding forward until I was practically on top of the man, I extended my right hand. "Hello, Caiaphas. My name is Lucius Pontius Pilate. Emperor Tiberius has appointed me the new Prefect of Judea."

CHAPTER SIXTEEN

We had been traveling for two weeks and three days and I could sense a change in the air that could only mean we were getting close to Delphi. I knelt on the wooden bench of the carriage to extend the upper half of my body out of the small, high window.

"Claudia, get down from there or—"

Just as the words left Sabina's lips, the carriage jolted to the side, tipping about forty-five degrees. I tumbled out the window and landed on my head hard. *We must have hit a sizable boulder.*

I was lying next to the carriage with several good-sized sharp rocks digging into my back. I blinked several times to try and make Sabina's four eyes turn back into two. As I started to sit up, I felt a hand press me back down from behind. It was not Sabina's for she stood in front of me.

"*Damnum...despoinis mou!* I fear you have suffered damage to your brain...perhaps a concussion. If you check the back of your head, you'll feel a very large, and I suspect painful swelling. One that is growing. Please take your time rising. If you'll allow me to assist you..."

I recognized the voice. It was the soldier I had helped with the lame horse, addressing me in both Greek and Latin.

Unusual, I thought.

Taking his advice, I accepted his strong hand and rose very slowly. The world spun, and I fought back nausea. "You're an *aesculapia*?" I asked. It seemed clear from his remarks that the fellow had some type of medical training. Although I tried to focus on his answer, all I could hear was the sound of hammering—like an anvil on iron. What had begun as a minor headache was fast becoming all-consuming. The soldier's face was close enough to mine that I could see the stubble on his chin. His mouth was moving, but, for the life of me, I could not understand what he was saying. His face was spinning...he had four eyes....

I glanced back at the carriage, which remained on its side. Several soldiers seemed to be laboring over one of its wheels, which had clearly been badly damaged.

My aunt and uncle were nowhere to be seen, though, granted, just turning my head to look for them caused a distracting, fiery pain. I closed my eyes for just a minute...and when I opened them, the pain was gone.

It seemed as if mere minutes had passed, but I no longer lay on rough stones. I was in bed. A real bed. Carefully, I moved my head to see if the pain would return. When it did not, I cautiously rose to a sitting position and was surprised to find that I was in my nightclothes.

Where am I?

Cautiously, I swung my legs over the side of the bed, stood, staggered a little, then steadied myself. I walked gingerly over to a good-sized window, which was shuttered against the sun. I unlatched the shutters and opened them wide, but no sun came in—just chilly mountain air. It was past nightfall. I had been asleep for much longer than a few minutes.

When my eyes adjusted, I could see the peaks of Mount

Parnassus in the moonlight. I imagined that I could see the oracular shrine at Delphi and hear the song of the underground river at the Castalian spring, though it was not really possible to do either at that moment. I felt as if I could stand in front of that window, breathing that hyper-oxygenated air for the rest of my life.

I was home.

Claudia, breathe deeply. Make this last. Bathe each cell in the sacred air, and store up enough of it to last the rest of your life.

I was just fifteen. How could I possibly know then that I would come back to this place? That I would die here, like an animal returning to its den?

CHAPTER SEVENTEEN

I jumped at the sound of Sabina's voice. It was dark in the room, and I saw only her shadow through a doorway of what must have been an adjoining room. "Sorry, Aunt, I didn't hear what you said," I managed.

The lamp she carried illuminated her anxious expression. " I'm so relieved to see you up, Claudia. How do you feel? Are you dizzy? I wonder if I should go get Gracian….He said to call for him when you awakened."

In a rush, I remembered what had happened and explored the back of my head with my right hand—and winced when it found its objective. "Gracian?"

Sabina entered the room and placed her lamp on a table next to my bed. "Gracian is the legionary medic who brought you here—he and the others fashioned a litter to transport you. I walked beside you to make sure you remained still..." Her voice cracked.

They must have thought I was dying!

"I...I can't remember the trip," I stammered. "The last

thing I remember is closing my eyes against the pain…It couldn't have been for more than a few minutes."

"That was three days ago, child. You've been sleeping quite a long time. When Gracian roused you to check your eyes, you could stay awake for just a few minutes before falling back into a deep worrisome slumber. He was quite concerned about how your eyes behaved when exposed to bright light, actually… worried that you'd suffered a serious brain injury. Claudia, please get back into bed, I need to call Gracian and Adrian and let them know you are awake." She started toward me then stopped to stare at me in the dark, her left hand worrying the edge of her lower lip. I had seen her do that only a very few times. Her sense of relief was audible in her exhalation. "The gods have answered our prayers, Claudia," she sighed.

Turning back toward the table, she picked up the lamp she had placed there. The light made me squint, but I could see that her hand trembled violently. Although my head was beginning to pound in perfect harmony with my heartbeat, I could see the toll this ordeal had taken on Sabina. The dark smudges under her eyes looked like bruises, and I guessed that she had slept little since the accident, if at all.

"He feared that you would need trephination—a hole cut in your skull and bone removed to relieve pressure around your brain. But Gracian had never attempted such a thing; only seen it done on the battlefield, and was understandably apprehensive."

The things my aunt was telling me…it seemed as if she was talking about someone else. *Cutting a hole in my skull? Removing bone?* I was having trouble processing it. My thoughts were jumbled. I knew I was staring stupidly, but could not think of anything to say. Finally, I managed to get out, "Three days?... I have been asleep for all that time?" *Sleep* was probably not the proper term for it.

I wished desperately that Antonia were here with me. In my mind, I could feel her cool hands on my head. When I was a child, it was Antonia who brought down my fevers and eased my various maladies. A slave from her early teen years, she'd worked exclusively for Sabina and Adrian, and undertook my care from the beginning. Her Greek was only passable, but she was a born teacher and the reason I spoke fluent Gallic.

I had not asked if Antonia could accompany me into this new life. I'd felt the mere question would seem presumptuous at worst, unseemly at best. Now, I wished I had asked, on that early morning when I learned we were going to Delphi. I could feel tears forming and swiped at my eyes, hoping that Sabina would not notice. *Don't be a baby, Claudia.*

But I needn't have worried. My aunt's gaze was trained on the doorway through which she had come a few minutes earlier. Uncle Adrian was standing there with a soldier, who preceded him into the room in a commanding fashion. This, I assumed, was Gracian. He strode over to the window where I stood as if nailed to the floor, took my hand and led me gently, but firmly back to bed.

Ah yes, the soldier with the lame horse. He must be Gracian.

"You are better, that is evident...but just twenty-four hours ago, your condition was much more dire. So serious that I was concerned I'd have to shave that lovely hair off your head and drill a hole into it! You must rest."

"She needs to eat something," said Sabina. "It's been three days...."

"Soup and perhaps a few bites of toasted bread for now," Gracian replied. "No more. Her system needs time to come back to life."

Even Adrian didn't presume to direct Sabina—but she nodded obediently at the medic and left the room.

Looking back at me, now safely back in bed, Gracian smiled. "The boss would not be happy if I let anything happen to his bride."

"Do you mean you work for Lucius Pontius Pilate?" I tasted the words as I spoke them. I liked the sound of his name. It was the first time I had said it.

Chuckling, he glanced at my uncle. "Yes, that is precisely who I work for."

Adrian smiled and walked over with a glass of water and placed it on the table. "Doctor's orders, Claudia. You need to drink."

Gracian waited while I drank the water, then, taking the lamp that Sabina had left on the table, ushered Uncle Adrian before him through the door, gently closing it behind them.

CHAPTER EIGHTEEN

CAESAREA
Lucius Pontius Pilate

Grasping my hand, the priest said, "Hello, Lucius Pontius Pilate. Yes, I am Caiaphas. The high priest here in Judea."

Without letting go, he drew closer and studied me openly. The crowd drew closer as well. This must have been the most exciting thing that had happened all week. Maybe all year. Other than a few stray murmurs, the vast throng had quieted. The desert air felt electric, charged with energy.

As I met the priest's gaze, I thought about how alien I must look to these people. The new Roman Prefect of Judea, dressed as a legionary soldier, standing alone, unguarded, unprotected.

The women, many accompanied by children or holding them in their arms, were veiled. I presumed that their presence outside was unusual, marking the significance of the moment. The men stood in groups, openly curious and eager to overhear any snippets of conversation between their High Priest and me. All wore loose, woven robes and lengths of the same fabric wrapped around their heads. The men all had beards.

Beards. I stared back at the hirsute face regarding my unshaven one. Without thinking, I lifted my left hand to scratch my jaw, but stopped my hand in mid-air, extending it outward instead and then moving it slowly back and forth, as if I were blessing the city. I could almost read Caiaphas's mind as his intense, almost black eyes peered defiantly at me. *Is this man a fool? Or reckless? Or... courageous?* He seemed to wonder.

I wondered myself.

Sejanus had spent considerable time and effort in promoting a ploy to make me look weak in the eyes of the Judeans. For many weeks, I had ruminated about the reasons for this and concluded that I'd never fully understand his motives. But the failed gambit did serve to underscore the importance of establishing myself immediately and firmly as a ruler with the prerogative of the Emperor.

Judea was one of our newest and most refractory provinces. I knew the Jews believed themselves to be superior in every way to all other nations—even the Roman Empire. They were a *chosen* people, they insisted; chosen by a god who had dictated to them rules of behavior, diet, morality, every aspect of their lives. Even more troublesome, they were not confined to Judea. There were Jews everywhere now, in every nation, and their numbers were growing. A significant conflict with Rome would bring hundreds of thousands of them into the tiny province of Judea, with the potential to overwhelm the five thousand men at my command.

The place was a powder keg. Every legionnaire knew it, and I had heard stories about the missteps of my predecessors. These people had been enslaved for most of their existence and had no reason to expect better than contempt, disrespect, and brute force from Rome. It would be important to confound their expectations.

I thought of Cicero's writings on civil service, which I'd

brought with me on the journey:

> *It takes a brave and resolute spirit not to be disconcerted in times of difficulty or ruffled and thrown off one's feet, as they say, but to keep one's presence of mind and one's self-possession and not to swerve from the path of reason. Now, all this requires great personal courage; but it also calls for great intellectual ability by reflection to anticipate the future, to discover some time in advance what is going to happen, whether for good or ill, and what must be done in any possible event, and never to be reduced to having to say, "I hadn't thought of that."*

That I had taken Cicero's ideas to heart was the reason I stood here alone. If I was to be taken at my word—that I was not just Rome's chief soldier in Judea but the chief magistrate and head of the Judean judicial system—I had to embody the role. This could not be done by hiding cravenly behind my soldiers.

If this priest believed it, so would his followers.

After what seemed like a lifetime—but was probably just about three minutes—of staring into the bold and penetrating gaze of Caiaphas, I spoke. "Your city, this harbor, is more beautiful than I could have imagined," I said evenly, working hard to maintain equal footing with this man. Although the offensive statue of Caesar Augustus loomed to my right, my back was to it.

At the sound of my voice, Caiaphas's hairy jaw worked and his coal-black eyes danced. The priest was smiling. He placed his free hand on top of our clasped ones, then broke free and raised both fists in the air, shouting in flawless Greek, "This is Lucius Pontius Pilate, the new Prelate of Judea…whom I accept. With whom I will partner to keep our faith and families secure." He then repeated what he'd said in Hebrew.

A resounding cheer arose from the assembled crowd.

CHAPTER NINETEEN

DELPHI

Claudia Procula

After close to a week of enforced bed rest, it was decided that I was well enough to continue our journey. It was a mere five-hour ride to the sanctuary at this point. Dutifully, I sat on the bench of the carriage, never once rising to look out the window. I felt a strange combination of emotions ranging from extreme gratitude to dread. That I had come very close to death was evident, and so was the fact that my own carelessness had been at least partially to blame for the mishap. But, the timing of our collision with the massive boulder seemed, well…somehow orchestrated. As seriously injured as I had been—and I fully believed Gracian's word on that—here I was. Back to full health. It felt to me as if I had been dropped into a vortex of opposing forces, one purely malevolent, and managed to come out the other side. I had no doubt that the fulcrum of the chaos was my future husband.

As I pondered the matter of my fate, I felt the weight of Sabina's regard. I looked over at my aunt, who had regained her usual glow and vigor right along with my own return to health.

But at this moment she looked grave as if reading my thoughts.

I smiled broadly. "Oh, Aunt, forgive my serious demeanor. I have just been thinking about the fact that in under six weeks, I will be a wife. My life is about to undergo so many changes. These are normal jitters for a bride-to-be, are they not?"

Quickly, she exchanged her frown for an answering smile. We'd agreed to our mutual fiction.

The very next moment, we slowed and stopped; we had arrived in Delphi. Once we had alit the carriage—without thinking—I sprang the short distance between Sabina and myself and knelt at her feet on the sacred ground. "Oh, Aunt, how can I thank you for bringing me back to this place? How can I make up for all of the worry and sacrifice that my presence in your life has caused you?"

My aunt pulled me to my feet so that we stood almost nose to nose. "Claudia, you have nothing to make up for. Nothing. And coming back here to Delphi is not just a favor to you; it is a blessing for Adrian and me as well. We have not been back here since we came to bury Amara and…collect you." Her expression remained composed and serene as she continued. "Her spirit sleeps here, Claudia. Your mother awaits you—out there." As she gestured toward the magnificent Temple of Apollo on the mountainside, tears shimmered in her eyes like jewels. "Go, child. Take as long as you like here."

She knew as well as I that the Oracle accepted supplicants only on the seventh of each month. Due to my injury, the seventh of October had come and gone twenty days prior.

CHAPTER TWENTY

CAESAREA
Lucius Pontius Pilate

"Another risky gamble, Lucius." Quintillus arrived just as the crowd was dispersing. I thanked Caiaphas for his support and agreed to join him at his home for dinner two days hence.

Shaved, bathed, and sensibly dressed in a white toga, Quintillus looked a decade younger than his fifty years.

"Yes, but it paid off, my friend," I replied, not bothering to hide my self-satisfied smile.

We walked north from the promenade to the palace. My palace. I had a hard time thinking of it as such, but I supposed I'd get used to it. Summer still maintained its hold on this coastal city, while it was fall by now, I was sure, back home in Rome. *Home? Certainly, Rome was not that to me. I'd spent only a few years of my life there, in school and legionary training. Where, in fact, WAS home?*

Quintillus hadn't responded to my retort, but I knew his thoughts as if they were my own. *There will come a day...*

The heat of the midafternoon sun was intense as we strolled up the steep road leading to the palace. As we passed by

a succession of blinding-white stone houses, we could see curtains move. The Caesareans were inside, wisely avoiding the
blazing sun, but that didn't stop them from tracking our progress.

Quintillus finally spoke. "One day, Lucius, I fear that
Fortuna will favor another who catches her eye. She is fickle,
this goddess of good fortune."

Choosing to ignore his typical brooding, I looked off to
the right and saw the Hippodrome. "Magnificent," I murmured,
slowing down to let my gaze linger. "It's hard to believe, but it
looks as large as Circus Maximus in Rome."

As I'd hoped, Quintillus let go of his portentous train of
thought for the moment. I had had enough premonitory musings
of my own about this land, these people, and my entry into
Roman politics. I knew I was wearing my legionary uniform for
the last time but was working hard to ignore this reality. I had
left all that I knew and loved and strived for, for…what? State-
craft. About which I knew less than nothing.

For the previous five years, I'd gone into battle knowing
that each day might be my last. There were times when I was
sure of it. I had expected to die in battle. Nobly. Honorably. But
it seemed now that fate had something else in mind for me. That
period of my life was over. The new brand of warfare I'd be engaged in was one of wits, verbal maneuvering, and deception.
This was Sejanus's form of combat, and the priests', too. They
were well trained in the use of words as weapons and understood
the art of manipulating their superiors as well as their followers.

My ploy with Caiaphas had worked almost too well. I
was unnerved at just how consummately I had earned his support.

Nodding at Quintillus's unspoken entreaty that we make
haste, I quickened my pace—but the activity did little to mitigate
my disquiet.

*Lucius, would you be happier if they had stoned you? If
you were lying on the promenade bruised, bleeding, or dead?*

Perhaps I would.

For now, these people were my allies—but I knew it would take just a whisper to awaken their enmity. I suspected that Caiaphas could incite murderous rage among these Hebrews if he chose to do so, and direct it squarely against Rome and me.

Theirs was a religious fervor I could not grasp. I had made the requisite sacrifices to Mars, just as all legionnaires did, since my childhood days. But, did I honestly believe in this deity and his power to protect me? Did I believe in the others, with their specific powers and causes? The truth was, if I embraced any religion at all, it was Stoicism. My Greek tutors had schooled me in the writings of Xeno and Epictetus. Foundational to me was the belief that, through the forces of will and discipline, I could control my own affections, opinions, bodily appetites, and the like. And, when it came to the things outside of my control— the things controlled by the opinions of others such as position and prestige, or matters of illness and death—I resigned myself to accept what came my way with equanimity. With every cell of my being, I knew that it was my own mastery of myself that had effected the truce with Caiaphas—not the will of a remote god.

Of late, I had discovered the work of a young Spaniard named Seneca, also a Stoic, and had gone so far as to write to him, advising that I had memorized a passage of his I admired:

> *The sovereign good of man is a mind that sub-jects all things to itself, and is itself subject to nothing: his pleasures are modest, severe, and reserved: and rather the sauce or the diversion of life than the entertainment of it. It may be some question whether such a man goes to heaven, or heaven comes to him: for a good man is influenced by God himself, and has a*

kind of divinity within him. What if one good
man lives in pleasure and plenty, and another in
want and misery? It is no virtue to contemn su-
perfluities, but necessities: and they are both of
them equally good, though under several cir-
cumstances, and in different stations.

I was delighted when he replied, and thus began our cor-
respondence. Although over a decade my junior, Seneca seemed
a kindred spirit. He informed me that he planned to return to
Rome imminently, as his writings were beginning to attract faith-
ful followers there—myself among them.

In spite of the self-confidence that my beliefs engen-
dered, I understood—just as Quintillus did—that there would
come a time when I reached into my bag of tricks, only to find
it empty.

"Lucius, welcome to your new home!" Quintillus said expan-
sively. He stood on the bottom step leading up to the portico of
the grand edifice, his right arm extended straight in front of him
in a salute.

I had been so immersed in my musings that I had barely
looked up as we approached the immense palace. I saw now that
it that made even the Emperor's residence in Rome seem hum-
ble. Built on a promontory overlooking the restless Mediterranean Sea, it was lined with columns in the Greek Doric
style—too many of them to count, it seemed. I could scarcely
take in the entirety of the structure, as it filled my vision from
end to end and beyond.

I glanced over at Quintillus, friend of my heart, to find
him sporting a rare smile. "What do you think your bride will
think of her new home, Lucius?"

CHAPTER TWENTY-ONE

CASTALIAN SPRINGS, THE SHRINE AT DELPHI
Claudia Procula

The kaleidoscopic images and voices were mostly indecipherable—a montage of visions and murmurs. Then, one female voice rose above all the rest. *Could it be the last Oracle? Or am I imagining her, because I need so desperately to hear her voice?*

As I lifted my gown and stepped carefully in, I found the water shockingly cold and the current rapid. The cold seemed right, though; proper. In spite of the constriction of my garments, I had no trouble negotiating the crevices, fissures, and sharp rocks....It was as if I knew every hairpin turn. Like a creature of the depths, I became one with the stream, the rocks, the cavern. It was almost as if I could breathe while submerged, like a fish or other underwater creature. I needed to surface only rarely. No conscious thought regulated my movements or the steady strokes of my limbs. Something had taken control of me—a force both alien and familiar.

I had taken Sabina up on her generous offer upon our arrival at the shrine, and had sprinted off to the Castilian Spring. Although I had not swum since early childhood, with my mother—some twelve years ago—I found that its exertions were better known to me than was walking. The activity took no effort at all. It was automatic—like breathing.

Images revealed themselves to me at an astonishing rate. Some were clearly faces—not Greek or Roman, but exotic. Bearded men, veiled women, small children came up in successive, flashes, their particulars as clear to me as if I were remembering them, but of course that couldn't be. These people were of a race I did not know. Many of their expressions revealed rage, murderous intent—but I felt no fear at seeing them. Rather, I sensed that I was being prepared for something.

Along with the exotic likenesses came those of my beloved intimates, including my mother, whose face I couldn't possibly remember and yet I knew it was she. There was the jutting crag of Mount Parnassus, reluctantly giving way to the Phaedriades—the twin "Shining Rocks" that had acted as the womb of Delphi, glistening like marble does in the morning sunlight and turning to liquid gold in the setting sun. The flashes were kaleidoscopic and outside of time.

Exquisite and elaborate temple columns rose high enough to kiss the gods, contrasting crazily with the gray wildness of the sheer mountain cliffs behind. I experienced memories of the infused wisdom I'd received as a child—but they were less like recollections than impressions of unseen realities, truths, and absolutes.

I swam in the soul of Sophia.

I desired only this.

Precisely at the moment I became aware of experiencing bone-chilling cold so severe that my teeth and entire body shook uncontrollably, strong warm hands reached through the top of the cavern and pulled me into the chamber of the Oracle.

Many hands wrapped me in warm blankets and brought me to a raging fire on the floor of the vast cavern of the Temple of Apollo.

"Claudia, daughter of Amara, welcome home."

The speaker was a woman considerably older than my aunt, her matronly face so lined and fissured that she seemed a facsimile of the mountains that served as a backdrop for this sacred place.

Through chattering teeth, I asked, "Are…you…Sophia? Or…my mother…Amara? Do I know you?"

My voice echoed off the rocks and came back to me sounding strange, shrill. The woman—she had to be the Oracle—said nothing. Like the six other women gathered around me, she was dressed in a long linen gown.

Without thinking, I fell to my knees, sobbing. I had no idea why.

Was it in reverence of this woman? Did I think she was my mother? Or was I simply overwhelmed by the pure joy of being *here*—where I belonged?

The Delphine air was my breath, these rocks more a part of me than my own hands, toes, or eyes.

The women watched and waited as I wept, their stillness and patience mirroring the great stones of their home.

When, finally, I quieted, the woman who seemed the quintessence of wisdom began to speak. The others gathered in a circle around her.

CHAPTER TWENTY-TWO

CAESAREA
Lucius Pontius Pilate

I wandered through the palace, alone for the first time since waiting for Tiberius to receive me. After a quick tour and introduction
to the twenty-five servants who took care of the immense structure, Quintillus left to return to his barracks and soldiers. How
he had learned and recalled all those names was a mystery to
me—but, then again, he knew most names of the eight-hundred
soldiers, forty-three slaves, servants, cooks, and medical order-
lies that comprised the century. I knew the names of maybe
twenty of them, those who had been with us since the first Germania battle. In my new position, I would have to attend more
closely to such details; all eyes would be on me. Even at that moment, I could sense the scrutiny of the staff as I ambled along,
delighting in my solitude and a momentary reprieve from obligations.

     Herod had selected a perfect spot for his monument to
Augustus. The palace sat atop a promontory that provided spectacular views of the pounding Mediterranean surf to the west and
the alabaster city to the south. As I wandered along the portico

of the second floor, the breeze from the ocean enveloped me, startling in its coolness. Abruptly, I sensed a presence behind me. When I turned around, I saw a man whose teeth shone stark white against his almost-black skin.

Of all of the introductions Quintillus had made, I had remembered just one name: that of this Egyptian, Sabu. Not much older than I, Sabu had worked at the palace since he was a boy and knew each corner of the place.

"May I show you the palace in more detail, Your Excellency?" he asked diffidently, his eyes downcast. This was the proper attitude of a slave, although Quintillus had told me that Vitellius had freed the man when he'd promoted him to head of the household some years before.

Thinking of my upcoming wedding—just one month away now—I nodded and replied, "Yes, Sabu. I recall a large dining area...I think it would be fitting for a wedding celebration, would it not?"

"Yes, Excellency," he replied. "I will take you to it now."

Upon my second perusal of the room, I could see that the dining room could seat one hundred, at least—but every nook of it was crowded with jeweled plates, chalices, glittering gold mirrors, and chandeliers. Dozens of oriental rugs obscured what was clearly a beautiful mosaic floor. The effect was overwhelming and...garish. There was no other word to describe it.

Sabu must have had a touch of Quintillus's clairvoyance. "We can adjust the furnishings as you wish, *excellentiae vestrae quantas*." His Latin was remarkably accurate and his pronunciation exceptional. Without thinking, I laughed.

Sabu's expression darkened. Too late, I realized that he might interpret my laughter as a judgment on his facility with Latin, or the words he'd chosen in salutation.

I reached out to touch his arm, but stopped at the last moment, having no idea what such a gesture might imply. Although among Romans, sexual contact between men—and particularly with male slaves—was considered acceptable, the thought of it repulsed me. There had been rumors of Herod's interest in very young males near the end of his life, and Sabu would have been just the right age to catch his eye when he first came to the palace. I suppressed a shudder at what slaves and their children were forced to endure.

"Sabu…I'm afraid you misunderstand. I laughed in surprise at hearing my own language—and spoken so well! Please, take no offense."

He was tall, nearly my height, and as thin as a reed. At my apology, his rigid posture relaxed, but only slightly. Sabu still did not meet my gaze. Instead, he looked down and to the right as if the elaborate mosaics in the tile floor held secrets.

"I am intrigued by your comment," I continued. "What adjustments to the room might you have in mind?" Moving swiftly through the cluttered space, I indiscriminately touched a variety of objects. Some wobbled dangerously in my wake. "Could we perhaps move this...and this...and all of *these*?"

Sabu suppressed a smile, and in his response, downgraded his salutation from *Your Excellency*. "Sir, if I may make a suggestion?"

"Indeed you may—I'd welcome it."

"I know you have been traveling for close to thirty days. Allow me and a select few other servants to help me transform this dining area to your pleasure." This time, his piercing dark eyes met mine. "I believe you prefer simpler furnishings that might highlight the spaciousness of the basic architecture—is that correct?"

I stared at him. Until then, I'd not analyzed the reasons for my distaste, but he was absolutely correct. There were large double doors on all four walls that opened up to a porch that wrapped around the entire room. Each presented a stunning view of the surf pounding the walls encircling the palace. But these aspects were lost amidst the clutter.

I nodded slowly. "Yes, Sabu. That is precisely what I am looking for."

"Very well, sir. I will see to it. May I direct the cooks to prepare you a late lunch?"

His smile was a shade less obsequious than before. I recalled the well-known maxim that Rome's enemies precisely equaled its current population of slaves. Perhaps I could win this one over.

"Sabu, somewhere I recall seeing a pool. A freshwater pool?" At his answering nod, I beamed. "Lovely. I will take a swim and bathe. I would guess there are new tunics and robes in my quarters? If you could ask someone to bring it to the pool, then yes, a late lunch would be excellent."

CHAPTER TWENTY-THREE

Wordlessly, I stared at my aunt and uncle. I was overcome.

Pretending she could not hear us conversing, Antonia discreetly continued packing the last of the numerous bags and parcels that we would take the next day as we sailed from Athens to Caesarea.

"Claudia, Adrian and I are delighted to include Antonia in your dowry. And when we spoke with her last evening, she seemed happier than I have seen her in months. You should know, Claudia, that this service to you is Antonia's choice. She was freed more than fifteen years ago."

This surprised me—not the news of Antonia's status as a free woman, but the fact that my aunt chose this moment to tell me of it. Perhaps it was one more of her attempts to make up for lost time.

For just a moment, Antonia's busy hands stopped their constant motion and lay like downed birds atop the pile of togas. Her back was to me, but I sensed her sudden attention. On the very top of the stack of garments was a bright red chiton, carefully folded. My wedding dress.

Sabina spoke into the silence. "No need, to say anything else, Claudia. Adrian and I could not be happier for both of you."

The wringing of Sabina's hands belied her positive tone. I knew she was distraught at the notion of my sailing to Caesarea with just Antonia to meet the stranger betrothed to me five years before. Perhaps she was also considering how empty the house would seem without me, after all of my years in it.

Since our reconciliation, my aunt had not hidden her sense of regret over our estrangement—the time she'd wasted in anger when we might have become close. It was true…we'd lost years when she could have taught me about the mysteries of men, women, and love. But, although she was quick to acknowledge her remorse, I understood that it wasn't her fault alone: When I thought back about the type of child I had been, I had to admit that I'd have resisted any such conversation between us. But Sabina seemed incapable of sharing the blame or forgiving herself.

The Oracle had told me that my mother's sister possessed a melancholic nature—that she lacked the capacity for joy and the resilience needed to pursue happiness in this life. Whatever her nature, I knew only that I was overwhelmed by her kindness and generosity, as well as my uncle's. But I was anxious to begin this thrilling adventure, and to be on my own…at least for the few weeks until my life would be commandeered by my husband, Lucius.

I had Gracian to thank for my reunion with Antonia. We'd originally planned to travel directly from Delphi to Judea. Our return to Athens had been the result of the medic's insistence that I wait another two weeks before setting sail. He feared that my recent concussion could cause me unpleasant side effects on the voyage if I undertook it too soon. Thus, our return to Athens, accompanied by Gracian and the seven other cavalry officers.

I had been expected in Caesarea by the Roman feast day of Bona Dea—the goddess of chastity and fertility—on December 3rd. But my injury, the length of time I'd spent with the Oracle, and our unplanned return to Athens had consumed close to thirty days. I would be fortunate if our ship docked by the date of our wedding celebration, December 17th.

Just as Antonia closed the last of our parcels, I heard voices: Adrian's and Gracian's. My uncle entered the house first, strode over to hug me, and then swung me around the room. "Are you ready for the voyage to Caesarea, dear Claudia? How I wish Sabina and I could accompany you to one of the most beautiful cities in the empire." He was just a couple of inches taller than I, and my face was mere inches from his. I could see the genuine affection—love—and joy in his dancing gray eyes.

At the approach of Gracian, Uncle's expression sobered and he placed me carefully back on the floor. "No need to worry about my damaging the bride of the Prelate of Judea," he said in the direction of the medic.

Bride of the Prelate of Judea. The thrill at the sound of those words began at the top of my head and raced down through my body. Sabina rose from her chair and approached her husband, eyes brimming. Before she could utter a word, Adrian took her hand, patted it and said, "Love, we're not going to say goodbye. We'll see our Claudia again."

Had I known it would be the last time I would see Sabina, would I have behaved differently? Been more expressive or loving? Those are the sort of unanswerable questions we ask ourselves when looking back through the shadowy corridors of our lives.

CHAPTER TWENTY-FOUR

The busy days and weeks flew by as I found myself consumed with my duties. Sabu had proven his worth several times over—at least it seemed so to me. It was he who sat laboriously over the heavy taxation record books, assuring that the Emperor continued to receive his due from the Judeans. All I had to do was review his efforts, nod my head, and affix my signature to the receipts that accompanied the payments to Rome.

The meetings I had to endure were frequent and interminable. Caiaphas and his entourage were in the palace several times a week, mainly to complain about fellow Jews whom the High Priest deemed dangerous to Rome. I learned quickly that I was not expected to do anything more than listen to his harangues, then express my appreciation for his fidelity to the Empire.

It was becoming clear that Caiaphas had meant what he said on that first day; he seemed determined that we'd work together as allies. He and his fellow priests hated Rome, but they feared rebellion from the other sects more. When he invited me to accompany him to Jerusalem, I surprised him—and myself—by accepting. He chattered like an old woman throughout the three-day journey, but I found his barbed questions—designed to catch me off guard—oddly penetrating.

As we prepared to leave Jerusalem, he handed me a prettily decorated alabaster container and said obsequiously, "We are most grateful for the return of our religious authority during the reign of Valerius, Prelate. Can you convey our gratitude to Caesar?"

The jar I held contained money, I was confident of that. I suppressed a smile at the man's canniness. Money was the surest way to the heart of any ruler.

The priest was clearly well versed in the rules of taxation. Of course, like all oppressed peoples, he had to be. But the deference to Rome seemed contrived, and I said as much to Quintillus who made no comment.

Later, back in Caesarea, sitting alongside the pool, my thoughts turned to Claudia. I didn't even know if she could swim, but I had visions of this woman I had never met swimming here on a daily basis.

While a servant refilled our glasses with wine. Quintillus picked up the conversation we'd begun standing before the Jerusalem Temple. "Lucius, these people fight over everything. The Pharisees hate the Sadducees, and both despise the Samaritans. They have but one common enemy and that is Rome." He took a deep draught of wine, swallowed, and then surprised me with what he said next. "You are doing well, Lucius; Far better than I would have predicted in this new world of politics. Making friends with Caiaphas was essential, and I think you have accomplished it more swiftly and fully than even Valerius did."

"Thank you, my friend. I could not have done it without your good counsel."

"Lucius…these querulous people would take their toll

on even the most patient of men. For your sake, I look forward to Claudia's arrival. She will distract them for a while. In one sense, at least, these Jews are just like everyone else: they love to gossip. You and Claudia will provide an inexhaustible source of rumors, lies, and half-truths. As for you, my friend...I imagine your bride will distract you, too."

My smile broadened as he spoke. I had been putting thoughts of the wedding out of my mind. *My bride*—I could not recall how long it was since I'd been with a woman. A year? Two? I could not afford to think about the benefits of marriage... not yet. But, despite my best efforts as a Stoic, vivid image of the marriage bed began to appear in my mind. "Indeed, I *will* be distracted for quite a while," I murmured under my breath. I have no doubt that Quintillus heard the remark.

Sabu entered just then with a large array of small dishes. "I know you said no supper this evening, sir, but the cook and I thought these might appeal." The Egyptian placed the tray on one of the small tables that had migrated from the dining room. I was quite pleased with the look of it against the stunning terracotta mosaic floor, and the way the rubies and emeralds embedded in its gold filigree top reflected varicolored rays along the surface of the water. Once again, I thought of Claudia swimming here.

Since the pool was very long, about ten meters, there was ample room for several comfortable lounges, each with its own table, along its perimeter. I reclined on one and Quintillus another. Each of us accepted plates from Sabu, and within a few seconds, were ravenously dispatching the supper we'd claimed we did not want.

CHAPTER TWENTY-FIVE

PAPHOS, CYPRUS
Claudia Procula

"Antonia, do you see that man?"

As she turned to look, I placed my hand on her arm and whispered, "Wait! Don't turn around so obviously. He wears a white Roman toga like a Senator, but he is young—not much older than I. Every time I go up to the deck he is there as if waiting for me."

Our ship had been docked at Paphos for two days, and I was exceedingly grateful to walk on solid earth. The seas had been rough all the way from Athens—so much so that I had been able to ingest only tea and some bread. Worried that I would grow too thin for my husband-to-be, Antonia had suggested delicately that we find an inn with real Greek food. Toward that end, we strode through a busy and noisy public square filled with merchants hoping to sell their wares to disembarking voyagers.

"Have you told Gracian about this man, Claudia?"

"No…at first I thought his presence a mere coincidence, or a figment of my overactive imagination. But, here he is again—about six or seven paces behind us."

Antonia stopped at a vendor's stall and made a show of

examining a lace shawl, all the while discreetly glancing back from whence we'd come. As she smiled at the vendor, she murmured, "Yes, Claudia…I see the man you're describing. He's stopped at a booth a few meters behind us. Gracian and two of his men are right behind him. I think they are watching him watch us! Pick out one of these scarves, Claudia. Anyone of them would look lovely on you, and the activity of bargaining for it will give Gracian time to catch up. I'll attempt to signal him."

With that, she discreetly waved her handkerchief, hoping she'd caught Gracian's eye without alerting the stranger.

I was just finishing the purchase of the scarf when Gracian approached, frowning. "Claudia, is Seneca disturbing you? Has he made advances of some kind?"

Relieved and somewhat embarrassed, I smiled at his use of my first name. *Finally.* "Seneca…is that the man's name? Why…no, Gracian, he has never even approached me. It just seems odd that I seem to find him wherever I am. He seems to be following me."

Nodding, the earnest young soldier replied, "I'm sure he *is* very interested in you, Claudia, though not in the way you fear. Seneca is a renowned Roman Senator and orator. I was told by Quintillus that he has been corresponding with your husband for several months now and is on his way to see him in Caesarea. I have no doubt that he will be at your wedding celebration."

As he spoke, Gracian seemed to be examining my face for signs of any effects from the concussion. Automatically, I reassured him. "I'm fine, Gracian—really. I've experienced no double vision nor any nausea since leaving the boat. And what I felt as we sailed, well…I'm sure that even you must have been a bit ill with all the tossing and turning!"

Changing the subject to something more pleasant, I asked, "Will you join us for some dinner? We are in search of a traditional Greek restaurant…perhaps some acquacotta would satisfy us all." The medic had told me of his love of the dish, which his own mother had made by combining onions and chard in olive oil, frying them until brown, and then heaping the mixture onto fresh bread with liberal amounts of cheese. It had been his favorite meal growing up, and he lamented having not tasted it since he'd left home.

The thought of being able to eat without the necessity of holding tightly to our dinner plates for fear we'd lose them to the relentless rolling of the ship brought smiles to all our faces. The mysterious Seneca forgotten for the moment, we headed toward a welcoming inn.

CHAPTER TWENTY-SIX

"Suppose her concussion was worse than Gracian thought? And they had to turn back for surgical treatment somewhere?"

Claudia's ship was a day late, and there was no sign of any but merchant vessels on their way north and south.

Quintillus regarded me somberly. "Gracian is the best medic in the Legion, Lucius. I wish I had intercepted his message about the accident on the outskirts of Delphi...I would have spared you the worry. If you are this protective of a woman you've never met, by Jove, I have to wonder how you will behave once she has become your wife." Shaking his head, he continued, "Even in the worst battles we endured, I never saw you fret like this. I swear, Lucius—if you bring up her name again in the next hour, you and I are going to relieve Longinus and Agrippa on their security route through Caesarea tonight. The back streets in the middle of the night are where these new 'prophets' recruit followers...away from the careful daytime watch of Caiaphas and his religious police."

I stared at Quintillus, giving serious consideration to his

intended "threat." The distraction from worrying about Claudia worked well, playing directly into my desire to return to the far simpler days of combat when boundaries and enemies were clearly defined.

Uncharacteristically, Quintillus did not sense the direction in which my mind had wandered. As we stood side by side on the portico outside of the now elegant dining room, our eyes remained trained on the harbor. Lost in thought, tension suffusing his face and stance, he did not seem to see the ships before us.

"There is yet another prophet in Jerusalem that the Jews seem to be nattering on about," he said. "Apparently, this man eats only locusts and honey. He is drawing people to him from as far north as Tyre and Sidon to be baptized in the Jordan River."

I raised an eyebrow in my confidant's direction. "Baptized? In a river?" I knew *baptismum* to be a type of ritualistic washing, but immersion in a river was a strange practice unknown to me.

Finally, Quintillus turned to regard me. Without a hint of humor, he declared, "It's true, Lucius. This prophet claims that he is preparing the 'way of the lord.' He shouts, 'Repent! For the kingdom of heaven is upon us!' Long lines of Jews await the laying on of his hands and their immersion in the waters of the river Jordan."

"Do any of them come from Galilee?" That was Herod's territory, and I knew his answer would be *yes*. The chill I felt had nothing to do with the ocean breeze.

Herod Antipas was a caricature of his father. Out of courtesy, I had gone to his palace in Galilee to meet with him during my first month in Judea. Even in September, the hot desert sun had not released its grip on this torrid land, and I'd yearned for the crisp fall weather of Rome. To make matters worse, I could no longer travel on horseback. My new rank required journeying via horse-drawn *carpentum,* a wooden coach with just one window and two uncomfortable wooden benches. Even over a short trip of six hours' duration, it had felt unbearably warm and airless.

By the time we arrived at Herod's palace, I was in a churlish temper, snapping at my three young soldiers for asking such reasonable questions as whether we would be staying the night. Quintillus had offered to accompany me, but I'd demurred, thinking it a waste of his time. We'd not be staying in this place a moment longer than necessary.

If Herod's father's taste had been garish, his own could be called vulgar. The palace was immense, easily twice the size of the one in Caesarea—I still could not bring myself to think of it as *my* palace—and built on an elevated platform more than one thousand meters square.

The edifice was a facsimile of the Greek style of architecture. I counted twelve Doric columns, but there was probably twice that number—the sun was in my eyes as I observed them. The cornices were embellished with tiny, ornate figures in a variety of shapes and sizes. The palace's two main buildings were separated by a courtyard, through which I entered. To my left was a grove of trees, their leaves whispering in the slight breeze. At the sound of rushing water, I looked to my right to see a large bronze fountain with a massive marble statue of Poseidon. Torrents of water emanated from his mouth and from each tip of his trident.

I stood for a moment, transfixed by the display of bad taste.

"Enter please, Procurator."

The voice was high and thin. Looking up toward the entryway, I expected to see a female servant, but there stood Herod, corpulent body encased in a white toga with a wide gold belt. Upon his bald head sat a crown.

I returned his smile, even though his salutation had been an insult. His use of the title *Procurator* communicated his belief that his position ranked higher than my own within the political morass that constituted the Empire.

I can use you, my good "King."

Determined to prove himself a gracious host, Herod insisted I join him for a meal in his palatial dining room. I only barely suppressed laughter when, having been seated in this mammoth chamber, I watched Herod clamber awkwardly up onto a dais a few meters above the long dining table and sit on a golden throne overlooking the room. I had never witnessed such grandiosity. No Caesar had behaved like this in my presence. I found myself almost sorry for the silly little man.

The room itself was half again as long as the dining room at Caesaria, but without any sense of order. There were glittering tables, statues embedded with jewels, and oriental rugs strewn throughout the vast space—much as there had been at my own abode when I'd arrived, but on an even grander scale. The need to outdo his father was pathetically evident.

Each finger of both of Herod's chubby hands was bedecked in glittering precious-stoned gold rings, and he waved them about as he directed placement of the surfeit of food. Ten servants brought out immense portions of lamb, beef, and accompanying dishes. *This feast could feed most of my troops,* I thought, ironically, as the heat had rendered my own appetite virtually non-existent.

The prophet claims the marriage to his wife is incestuous.

I recalled Herod Antipas's wife, Herodias. Antipas had invited her to join us at the meal. She was indeed beautiful and had been married to Herod's brother when they met in Rome. I remembered the story of the nasty divorce and hasty remarriage with more than a little unease.

Neither Quintillus nor I said a word as we considered the likely effects of this new prophet.

CHAPTER TWENTY-SEVEN

CAESAREA

Claudia Procula

"Wait here until I come for you both."

Gracian deposited Antonia and me, along with our two lightest bags and my handheld pouch containing the coins of my dowry, at the aft of the ship's top deck. My heart was hammering, but I tried to smile nonchalantly as he bade us wait and retreated.

Perhaps noting my paleness, Antonia inquired, "Are you feeling alright, my lady?"

Gratefully, I looked over at her and noted that her brows were drawn together over her grave, dark eyes. In spite of her constant concern, I found her mere presence greatly calming. What a blessing it was that she had traveled here with me. *Thank you for that, Aunt and Uncle.*

Surprising myself, I grabbed her thin shoulders and hugged her, whispering into her sweet-smelling neck, "Yes, Antonia, I am quite fine—more so because you are here." Straightening up, I continued speaking with my confidante. "I suppose I am just nervous…frightened…about assuming the obligations of a wife. I understand that this man and I were betrothed by agreement between Uncle Adrian and him...five years ago." I swallowed a bout of nausea and pressed on, my anxiety evolving into panic as I spoke. "But now the time is *here*. And my mind is in turmoil. I keep repeating the ancient Roman marriage ritual, *Quando tu Gaïus, ego Gaïa* as if I am an actress in one of Sophocles' plays...It is just five words, but you would think it hundreds!" My voice quavered—I was perilously close to sobbing. "And...I am quite frankly frightened about the wedding *night*, Antonia. Will I know what to do? What will he think of me— this man I am told is such a great warrior? Am I pretty enough for him? Womanly enough? Perhaps you think my questions silly—girlish—but...I know so little of such things!"

Antonia stepped back to regard me, her long thin face now filled with warmth. She smiled rarely, but when she did her face grew radiant. "Oh, Claudia, my child. Forgive my impertinence for saying it, but...ever since I first saw you as a little Delphine orphan, I have loved you." She reached up to trace my face with two fingertips. "You are special, my dear one, touched by the gods. Yours is a beauty unlike any other woman's."

She had never spoken to me this way, and I wondered at the meaning of her words. Was she simply trying to calm my nerves, or was there some truth in what she said? Her heartfelt words restored in me a measure of confidence, enveloping me like a warm *peplos* on a chilly night.

Just then, Gracian reappeared amidst the crowd jostling for position to disembark. At the sight of his uniform, people stood back.

"Follow me now, please, ladies, and stay close."

People stared at us as we made our way through the throng. Their faces seemed impassively curious for the most part, though a few registered defiance in their expressions as Gracian passed with us in tow.

The steadfast medic held open the door of a waiting carriage while I climbed in, then did the same for Antonia, all under the watchful eyes of the crowd lined up along the promenade. I wondered what drew their attention. Was it us...or the man in the white toga—the friend of Lucius named Seneca—who was disembarking just behind?

I knew we must have ridden for fifteen or twenty minutes at the very least, but, having lapsed into a daze, it seemed that mere seconds had elapsed when we arrived and disembarked from the carriage. Standing at the bottom of the long staircase, I looked up at the magnificent white palace. It seemed to glow in the light of the setting sun, casting its golden rays upon the man who stood on the portico above.

My husband was taller than I'd expected and dressed quite simply in a white linen tunic and sandals. His legs were long and muscular. As I climbed the marble steps toward him, he began to descend, and we regarded each other with open curiosity. Was he handsome? I had to admit that he was. After a month of seeing only long-haired and bearded men, I was captivated by Lucius's cropped black hair and naked face. His aspect was strange to me—but enticing. I blushed when I imagined those lips on mine. The feel of his strong arms around me.

When he reached the halfway point of the stair, he stopped to wait. Intentionally, boldly, I climbed to stand on the step he occupied, forcing him to step back against the marble riser to accommodate me.

His eyes widened just a little in surprise, and suddenly, I felt no fear at all.

"Hello, Lucius. How delightful to meet you." It came out sounding as if I met husbands-to-be on a daily basis. I found myself standing on tiptoe to kiss his cheek, then thinking how much I liked doing that. Most of the men I had known—even Gracian—were no taller than I. Lucius moved his head and my lips inadvertently grazed his cheek, then landed on his lips. The thrill that coursed through me caused me to tremble.

As my betrothed reached out to steady me, he smiled warmly, and I took my first close look at his eyes. They were dark brown with amber lights.

I could lose myself in those eyes.

As if from a distance—though the crowd that had followed us from the dock was close by—I could hear faint cheering. Louder in my mind was the voice of the Oracle:

This is your new home. This is the man you will love for your entire life, the only man you will lay with and conceive. This stranger belongs to you.

I had turned one hundred questions over in my mind about this moment—about my future—but now all of them had been answered in a single gesture. I stood in Lucius's embrace as hundreds of eyes regarded us.

CHAPTER TWENTY-EIGHT

Lucius Pontius Pilate

Sabu and his cohorts had outdone themselves in decorating for our wedding ceremony, Saturnalia, and reception. I wandered into the now beautifully appointed dining room where, in just under two hours, the wedding would commence. At the far end of the spacious room was a large marble altar to Jupiter. A dried sheepskin was draped over the stone to signify the bloodless sacrifice we would make to the king of the Roman gods, Jupiter. On each side of the altar were five long candles to represent the ten *gentes* of the early tribal *curia*. I drew a breath in awe at Sabu's meticulous knowledge of the detail required for a *confareatte*—the traditional wedding ceremony for a public official.

The elegant pebbled mosaic floor was now wholly visible. Muted, dancing lights from a vast array of candles bounced off the tastefully arranged selection of statues, urns, and goblets. In the spirit of Saturnalia—which is a holiday of giving—amusing tokens would be bestowed on our guests; they sat in each crevice and corner of the room. Assorted bouquets and wreaths of flowers adorned the long table, which was set for one hundred.

At each place setting was a vase with a single long-stemmed, peach-colored rose. The double doors facing the ocean were held open by large casks of wine, thus permitting the mild breeze from the sea to play with the flames of the candles.

I took a deep breath of pure pleasure as I reveled in the perfection of the setting—so fitting for my future wife. *Claudia.* The lump in my throat grew at the thought of her long, almost black hair, arched brows, beautiful eyes. She was everything her uncle had promised and more. Not that I knew much about her yet…but that first sight of her, that first kiss had taken my breath away. She wore none of the agents most women employed to accentuate their faces—nor had she any need for them. Would I call her beautiful? I smiled to myself. The word was too superficial to apply to my Claudia. She simply radiated loveliness from every pore.

I had to remind myself that she was just fifteen, still a child in years. Yet she carried herself like a woman my own age, or even older. Her self-possession—her boldness—stunned me. I had been with numerous women in my life, but none had possessed that…what was it…provocativeness combined with innocence?

I sensed rather than saw Sabu. Turning around, I smiled at him as he hesitantly approached from the main house. "All is perfection, Sabu, thank you. This room looks lovelier than I could ever have imagined. I had no idea of the beautiful detail of the Bacchus mosaic hidden under all those oriental rugs."

Sabu smiled briefly, but it was clear that he had something on his mind.

"Sabu…what is it?"

"Sir, one of your guests is here and insists upon meeting with you…right away. I explained that you are readying for your wedding celebration, but he was resolute. He says he has brought a gift for you all the way from Rome by way of Athens and must present it personally before the celebration begins. Shall I summon the guards to escort him away?"

Before I could answer, a booming voice could be heard amidst the patter of many feet and muted voices attempting to stop him.

"Lucius. Pontius. Pilate. Prelate of Judea!"

Seneca. I had never heard his voice yet knew it could belong to none other. This was clearly the voice of an orator. I had completely forgotten that he would be here. Why…he must have been on the same ship as Claudia!

Framed by the two vats of wine in the portico doorway stood a tall, thin man in the white toga of the Roman Senate.

Well, this should be interesting. He can't be more than twenty-five years old, yet feels no compunction at barging into the home of the Judean Prelate.

Suppressing my mild annoyance, I strode forward to meet him. "You must be Seneca, sir. How generous of you to make your way here for our wedding. Thank you very much for coming."

Looking around nervously at the bevy of servants and soldiers who had gathered, for a moment he seemed speechless.

"This is my friend," I said, directing myself to the centurion. "He is an invited guest, and I ask you to make him comfortable in the north wing. He will be staying here with us for a while—won't you, Seneca?"

Piercing bright-green eyes seemed to take my measure—a startling contrast to his long dark curly hair. Abruptly, the Senator dropped his angular, planed face to my extended hand and kissed it. "What an honor, sir…Lucius. I would be more than pleased to accept your most gracious offer." Straightening, he reached into the folds of his toga and handed me a scroll. "My wedding gift to you and your bride is my latest dialogue: *Of A Happy Life*."

Once I'd accepted it, he spoke in a heightened voice, as if addressing the Senate. "Wisdom does not teach our fingers, but our minds. She teaches us what things are good, what evil, and what only appears so; and to distinguish betwixt true greatness and rot. She clears our minds of dross and vanity; she raises up our thoughts to heaven and carries them down to hell: she discourses of the nature of the soul, the powers and faculties of it; the first principles of things; the order of Providence: she exalts us from things corporeal to things incorporeal and retrieves the truth of all: she searches nature, gives laws to life; and tells us that it is not enough to know God, unless we obey him."

Bowing while simultaneously submitting to the soldier waiting to show him his quarters, Seneca shouted, "Lucius, I wish you and your bride, Claudia, a long and happy life."

With that, he allowed himself to be whisked away.

"So, Lucius…that is your friend Seneca."

I had been so spellbound by the audacity of the orator that I had not noticed Quintillus enter the dining room, resplendent in his dress uniform. Distaste was evident in his eyes as he looked down the veranda after the receding figure. Turning back to me, his demeanor changed. His usually impassive face was split nearly in two by a smile. "Lucius, accept my congratulations! Claudia is uncommonly lovely, and a fine young woman. I had a few moments to speak with her and—"

As if on cue, Claudia entered the room, stopping Quintillus in mid-sentence. I was instantly aware of no one but this child who had stolen my heart.

CHAPTER TWENTY-NINE

"*Zahra*," I intoned. "That is a beautiful name. Does it signify something in your native tongue?" I knew the woman standing before me was wife to Sabu, the Egyptian man who seemed to run everything in the large palace.

Lips curving upward, she replied, "It means *blooming*— as a flower does."

Forgetting what Antonia was occupied with, I tipped my head to peer up at the girl, causing my friend and serving maid to drop the plait of my hair they had just fashioned into an elaborate swirl. Eyeing Zahra's flawless olive skin, glossy black hair, and large kohl-accented dark-brown eyes, I smiled. "What a perfectly fitting—"

"My lady!" snapped Antonia. "If you could please sit still for just five more minutes?"

We were overwhelmed, Antonia and I. Gone was the calm certainty of the evening before, and in its place was massive insecurity, disorientation, and anxiety. The weight of this marriage—and the opulence of the celebration marking it—were simply too much to take in.

The previous evening, after the audacious public embrace I'd shared with my husband, Lucius had gently but firmly disengaged himself and taken my hand to lead me up the rest of the stairs, where thirty people stood waiting...apparently for me.

Lucius had introduced me to Sabu who, in turn, introduced me to Zahra and nine other serving women. Antonia and I were then promptly escorted to another wing of the palace a full ten minutes away. We climbed another set of stairs, and Zahra stopped in front of a set of ornate bronze doors decorated with intricately detailed friezes featuring the Greek goddess Athena Nike. Both scenes depicted her nude, perfectly proportioned body, but only one included her wings and crown of victory.

Sabina would love this place. It feels odd to be this far from Greece and yet dwelling in a palace of Greek architecture decorated with our gods and goddesses. This must seem an offense to the local Hebrews, no? Is it an intentional one?

I cut short my thoughts as Zahra opened the massive doors to reveal a vast space furnished with a large, comfortable-looking four-poster bed. Near it was a sitting area that led to a separate space for hygiene. Two doorways seemed to lead to connecting rooms, perhaps to accommodate servants. Scattered around the larger pieces of furniture were elaborate tables, chairs, lamps, and statues.

The table nearest the bed was loaded with a variety of ceramic trays containing olives, cheeses, and fruits, plus some sort of redolent meat—perhaps lamb. I knew I should partake in this meal, but sensed that my nerves would not permit digestion.

"Madame Claudia, these are your quarters," said Zahra gently. "We hope they are adequate." The other women remained silent, bowing their heads as she spoke.

I opened my mouth to attempt a gracious reply, as befit my new and overwhelming role.

Adequate for whom? A queen?

Instead, I found myself bursting into tears and, to my supreme humiliation, unable to stop sobbing. I could hear Antonia murmuring excuses.

"Madame Claudia is very tired...she has traveled a very long distance...Yes, she will be fine in the morning, no need to worry. All is in perfect order."

The women filed out without another word in my direction, and suddenly I was alone with my trusted friend in a suite three times the size of the house I grew up in.

In spite of myself, I slept dreamlessly in that most remarkably comfortable bed. And now, the moment I'd anticipated was approaching. The event about which I'd felt nothing but eagerness was now—inexplicably—filling me with terror.

As Antonia attempted my ablutions, I could not stop fidgeting. But when it came time for Zahra to apply kohl to my eyes and various unfamiliar pigments to my cheeks and lips, I managed a modicum of stillness. I wanted to be ravishing for my husband. I wanted to stoke the passion that our brief embrace had hinted at.

Antonia's widened gaze told me more than any mirror could: the cosmetics had enhanced my looks as they were meant to do. Patiently, she replaited the last chunk of my hair, and we were done. Carefully, the two women dropped the scarlet wedding chiton over my head, covering the lace tunic that had been Antonia's wedding gift to me. Antonia then brought out a fillet made of white lilies and placed it on my head like a crown. Stepping into the sandals Zahra had placed on the floor, I did feel like a queen.

As one, the two women held up their hands and smiled. "My lady," said Zahra, "you make a most beauteous bride for Pontius Pilate."

Antonia and I followed Zahra down the staircase and along a long central hallway that led into a courtyard I had not previously seen. We crossed the yard, ascended another set of stairs, and walked rapidly along the veranda where Zahra stepped back so that I might precede her into one of the most stunning rooms I had ever seen. As I entered and looked around, my fears began to melt into the mists coming off the ocean through its wide double doors.

By the time I had taken two steps into the room, Lucius was at my side, his expressive eyes filled with light. Leaning down, he breathed into my ear, "How beautiful you are, Claudia, my bride. Tonight, we will finish what you started on the steps of the palace."

His words seemed to draw all the strength from my legs, and I swayed visibly. In an instant, he'd wrapped his long arm around my waist to steady me and turned me toward a large altar to Jupiter. Standing beside me, he extended his left hand, I replied with my right, and our hands clasped tightly together.

I had studied the dextrarum iunctio and understood this as the sacred handclasp, the first of the ritual of confarreate fit for a Prelate. Without dropping his hand, I turned to face Lucius and declared, "Quando tu Gaïus, ego Gaïa"—literally, "When [and where] you are Gaius, then [and there] I am Gaia." The words felt wholly natural. I am bone of your bone, flesh of your flesh.

I had feared that this ancient ritual would feel foreign or contrived. I was not Gaia, and he was not Gaius, nor did I believe in Jupiter as the Roman analog to Zeus. I knew there was just one God and yet—standing there in the light of the ten candles that represented the ten *gentes* of the ancient Roman *Curia*—the ritual felt undeniably sacred. Resplendent in his uniform, Lucius's lead centurion—Quintillus was the name I recalled—approached us from the far right of the room carrying the cake of spelt that would be a bloodless offering to Jupiter. Placing it next to a dried sheepskin, he bowed to Lucius and then to me, then backed away from the altar. Lucius—now officially and forever my husband—broke off a piece of the cake and offered it to me. I started to drop his hand to accept it, but he tightened his grasp. Slowly, sensuously, he brought the cake to my mouth, separating my lips with his long, elegant fingers. As I accepted the morsel, chewed, and swallowed, he kept his eyes locked on mine. Heat coursed through my body as I watched Lucius take a bite of the cake, chew and swallow. But before I could follow my instinct and move closer to embrace him, he stepped away, his eyes dark, warm and teasing.

"Come, Claudia—my own! There are more than a hundred guests who want to meet the wife of Pilate."

CHAPTER THIRTY

CAESAREA

Lucius Pontius Pilate

"I left you alone for three days, Lucius, but I can do so no longer. We need to go to Jerusalem—right away."

Quintillus stood shifting from one foot to the other, awaiting my reply as I stared blankly at him, attempting to process his words. Belatedly, I realized he was dressed in full uniform.

"Lucius," he pressed, "according to Caiaphas, there is trouble brewing. He demands that we travel there to quell what he insists is an incipient riot. The priest expects to meet us at the Jerusalem temple by sundown."

Quintillus and I stood outside my bedchamber, where Claudia and I had been wrapped in each other's arms since the wedding celebration. It was just before sunrise.

I felt dazed as if I had been asleep for days. *Nothing could be further from the truth,* I thought, an inappropriate smile claiming my lips.

Quintillus attempted a smile in return, but it faded quickly, replaced by a grave expression. Urgently, he bade me,

"Go, Lucius. Bathe, dress, and eat something. I'll be back to collect you in one hour. The road into Jerusalem is taxing on the horses. If we leave shortly, we'll have time to allow them to rest and water them before the ascent."

"So…am I to assume we are about to face the band of Galileans Herod Antipas is so afraid of?"

We had taken a centuria—eighty of the cavalry and another fifteen in support and servants. For the first thirty miles, we had made excellent time, riding southeast along the plain of Sharon. For the sake of efficiency, I was traveling on horseback instead of in that hideously uncomfortable carriage, and I was very happy to be doing so.

We reached the fertile valley of Ijon shortly after noon and, per Quintillus's plan, gave the horses their rest and nourishment. I had not made the trek to Jerusalem on horseback before, but if Quintillus considered it taxing for the horses, it must be a grueling climb.

My trusted companion looked puzzled at my question.

"The instigators of this 'incipient riot' that must be quelled…are they Galileans, or…who? Exactly what is the reason for this taxing journey?"

Quintillus looked exasperated, confounded, and weary all at once. "Lucius, I don't believe there is really any trouble brewing at all. I believe Caiaphas is testing us."

"Then why the centuria? Why the urgency?" I thought fleetingly of my warm marriage bed; my glowing young wife.

"Because, Lucius, I can't be certain. There may well be bands of rebels threatening to do battle with us with their sticks and stones. I believe we have no choice but to trust Caiaphas— for the time being, anyway."

Quintillus's instincts had proved themselves correct countless times, and I was not about to question them now. I suspected that he was right about the cunning High Priest and his ruses, but I respected his desire to err on the side of caution.

My jaw tightened, and I could feel my teeth grind together. It was a habit I had developed over the years in battle when faced with situations over which I had little control, and it was a bad one, to be sure. I could feel the start of a headache that often followed.

Quintillus watched me, suddenly composed. "Vitriol and contempt are what the man expects from us, Lucius. Don't give in to them. Each of your predecessors treated Caiaphas and his ilk as inferiors. So far, you have shown him respect. Think of it as a tactic—the kind you'd use in battle."

His wisdom was compelling, and the sound of his voice calming. I had no idea if Quintillus had studied the Stoics, or whether he'd even heard of them, but he personified the kind of man I wished to be. Dignified, honorable, with iron-clad self-control.

I nodded. "Perhaps we are in a battle as we speak, Quintillus. You're right—we are wise to act as if we are."

"If I am correct in my thinking, Lucius, you should be grateful for the chance to practice your skills on this new kind of battlefield, where the weapons are rhetoric and fakery."

Of course, he was right. I was a soldier, as unskilled as a newborn babe in this new world filled with the likes of Sejanus, Caiaphas, and—

My thoughts were interrupted by the appearance of a tall, thin figure clad in the white toga of a Roman Senate, making his way along the riverbed toward where we sat on large rocks by the water.

"Quintillus, that looks like...it *is* Seneca! How is it that he is *here*?"

Raising an eyebrow, Quintillus smiled sardonically. "You invited him, my friend."

"How could I have invited him on a journey I did not know I would be taking?"

"Perhaps you don't remember...you and Seneca had a lengthy conversation at the wedding celebration. He told you how much he desired to see Jerusalem before returning to Rome. You agreed to bring him along if it happened that you traveled there while he was still in Caesarea."

Responding to my bafflement, he added, "Lucius, you'd had a great deal of wine."

At that moment, his typically knowing smirk annoyed me a little. "He told you this, I presume?"

"He did indeed, as I was readying the horses and supplies."

At that point, Seneca moved within our earshot, so I said nothing more. I stood and walked over to meet him.

"Lucius, please pardon me for approaching you; I know your mind is on other, more important matters. But...I wonder if I can send you some writings about managing the Jewish exiles. This is material I have compiled...my own thoughts and the work of others. Would you be amenable to looking at it?"

It seemed an odd proposal, and I stood silently for a moment, not knowing quite how to answer.

Lowering his voice, the philosopher stepped closer. "Perhaps you should know...I was raised by a very successful and wealthy father in Spain. Father sought out the best tutors for me, and the principle among them was a Jewish friend of my father's. I spent considerable time at his home and with his wife and daughters and learned a great deal about Jewish culture and their complex social and religious protocols. That knowledge could be beneficial to you as you work to determine the most effective methods of ruling these people."

Seneca continued speaking, elaborating on various aspects of Jewish life and expounding upon the reasons behind their peculiar religious beliefs. While listening to his persuasive rhetoric, I recalled the wordless disdain of Quintillus and Claudia and considered rejecting the man's offer. The two people closest to me had both seen something in this man that I could not yet discern.

Perhaps I should walk away...

But as I opened my mouth to refuse him, I found myself saying, "Thank you, my friend. You are right in presuming that when it comes to the Jews, I am a *tabula rasa*. I know little about them, and understand even less."

Seneca bowed. "Lucius, you shall have the materials within a month after I return to Rome." With that, he went off to join a group of nearby soldiers.

CHAPTER THIRTY-ONE

When he left me, I felt as though half of my body had been sev-ered and discarded. The feelings of loss and pain were exqui-site—as if my heart and soul were hemorrhaging.

Our coupling had been far more than physical, and yet the physical had been the catalyst. The way our bodies fused was utterly astounding, igniting fires in the private places of my body I had never taken notice of.

That first night, alone in his bedroom as husband and wife, Lucius had been more nervous than I, touching me chastely at first, as if we were brother and sister.

"Shall I be the one to finish what I started on the steps?" I'd said, surprising myself with my own boldness. I had stripped off the chiton and stood to face him clad only in the lace tunic. Standing there with my hands on my hips, teasing and laughing, I'd felt alluring for the first time in my life. Beautiful and...wom-anly.

The electricity between us had been building throughout the evening. Whenever our hands had touched or our gazes locked, everything around us had seemed to recede into the background. We'd perceived only each other.

Lucius was more than twice my age and had been with many women before me, I knew this. He knew that I had never known another man, and was hesitant as to how to approach me. His physique was too big, too hard, too coarse. He was easily twice my weight and a good seven centimeters taller—and he was touchingly concerned about frightening or hurting me. I had no doubt that if I'd exhibited the least bit of fear or apprehension, we would not have consummated our marriage that night. But I'd felt neither of those.

Laying alone in my marriage bed, I thought back several years to my first encounter with a discussion about love in Plato's *Symposium*. At thirteen, I'd bragged to my uncle that I had wholly grasped the philosopher's meaning. Uncle Adrian had merely lifted an eyebrow.

"Uncle," I'd said, "you seem surprised that I have no further questions. Is it difficult to believe that I am capable of grasping this material?"

Uncharacteristically vexed, he'd replied, "Child, that allegory about the origin of humanity that Aristophanes offers when it is his turn to speak has ignited controversy ever since Plato first published the *Symposium*. Was Aristophanes jesting, as in one of his comedies? Or was his complicated conclusion that humans were originally split in half and are forever searching for their lost other half—their soulmate—meant literally, as a description of enduring human love?"

I could see him now, standing next to the couch where I sat, surrounded by pages of the scroll. He had just returned from his farm and was covered with the dust of the fields, obviously tired and rubbing his eyes.

Before I'd had the chance to respond, Uncle Adrian had continued very softly, "But Claudia, child of wisdom, how can I tell you what you do or do not understand?" Then, so quietly that I almost did not hear him, he'd added, "Now child, read Phaedrus. Perhaps you are ready for it at thirteen. I read it at twenty and did not understand any of Plato's words until just a few years ago."

I smiled at the memory of the child I was, at her purely intellectual comprehension of a thing that was fundamentally inexplicable: love. That sense of emptiness being filled— an emptiness you had not known was there. Love sure was kind of wholeness, completion, and—yes—the realization that you'd found your soulmate.

Soulmate. No wonder my uncle had been dumbfounded at my nonchalant reply. But then again, if I had asked for an explanation, would he have found the words? Per Uncle's suggestion, I had read Phaedrus next and thought now of Socrates' long discourse on the divinity of love and the madness it inspires. For there is no other word for this kind of love but madness, is there?

When he sees a godlike face or bodily form that has captured Beauty well, first he shudders, and a fear comes over him like those he felt at the earlier time; then he gazes at him with the reverence due a god...Once he has looked at him, his chill gives way to sweating and a high fever, because the stream of beauty that pours into him through his eyes warms him up and waters the growth of his wings. Meanwhile, the heat warms him and melts the places where the wings once grew, places that were long ago closed off with hard scabs to keep the sprouts from coming back; but, as nourishment flows in, the feather shafts swell and rush to grow from their roots beneath every part of the soul (long ago, you see, the entire soul had wings). Now the whole soul seethes and throbs in this condition. Like a child whose teeth are just starting to grow in, and its gums are aching and itching—that is exactly how the soul feels when it begins to grow wings. It swells up and aches and tingles as it grows them.

Aching and itching as my soul *grew wings*...YES! That is precisely how this felt, this sudden plunge into love.

Uncle Adrian, what a gift you gave me by immersing me in the writings of such learned men. This was the most precious of all bestowals: the kernels of wisdom.

When Quintillus had commenced knocking at the door of our suite, Lucius had groaned as if in pain. He had not wanted to resume his worldly duties any more than I had wanted him to. But, when it became clear that his friend was not going to leave us in peace, he roused himself and went to answer.

Guessing that servants would soon be coming in with hot water for his bath, I gathered my things, tossed them into a large pouch and slipped away to my own chambers while he and Quintillus were still talking outside. I knew that separation, as painful as it might be, was essential for us both. There was danger in being united so sublimely; if we'd continued without respite, our individualities could disappear. We could become something unhealthy—even unholy.

When my aunt and uncle had refused to say goodbye, I understood their meaning; we would see one another again, so there was no need for it. So it was with my husband. I would be out of his sight when he returned to get ready for his travels. We had no need for farewells.

While wandering back through the portico, I turned the wrong way and stood in an area of the immense palace I had not seen before. What lay before me looked like water. *Water inside the palace? How could this be?*

Getting close enough to see it clearly, I realized that it was some type of pool built by man. Squatting down, I tasted the water. Fresh, not salty. Inviting. *Precisely what I need to regain my wits.*

Glancing about to make sure no one lurked, I stripped off my peplos, leaving just my undertunic, and dove in. Finding even the tunic an impediment, I soon shucked it as well and began to swim hard. After just a few strokes, I sensed a sort of shimmering behind my closed eyes.

I was back at Delphi. Although the Oracle had predicted my return to the shrine, I had presumed she meant it literally; I would return to live there. But when I lifted my head above the surface of the shockingly cold water, I found myself swimming in the underground river of my homeland, Castalian Spring. I could see only the stone above me as my body was swept along by the swiftly moving subterranean current.

CHAPTER THIRTY-TWO

Pontius Pilate

It felt like Caesarea all over again. The streets were lined with people watching as we entered the city, the hooves of our horses echoing across the cobblestone streets. Two by two, our centuria rode down the narrow avenue, the retinue ending with Quintillus and me. But, while Caesarea was a quasi-Roman city, Jerusalem was Jewish at its core.

We had been riding for more than eight hours, and I was drained. Perhaps it was my imagination, fueled by fatigue, but it seemed to me that the tensions in this place were palpable, alive in the very air I breathed.

I had no expectation of being welcomed in Judea. I was, after all, the personification of its "oppression" by the Roman Empire. But the peaceful months in Caesarea had lulled me into thinking—hoping—that our long-standing enmities might ease under my tenure.

Although the ascent into Jerusalem was onerous, we'd been able to negotiate the paved road successfully through the pass of Beth-Horons, site of the infamous battle between Cestius

Gallus, legate of Syria, and the Judean infantry. Every soldier in the Empire had studied this ambush by the Judeans, as Gallus was withdrawing his soldiers to the coast to await reinforcements. I suspected that most of my eighty comrades were imagining the horrors that had taken place here just seventy-five years before.

Gallus's legion had been attacked by arrows fashioned into massive, flaming missiles by Judean scouts, then rushed by a large force of Judean infantry. Getting into formation had been impossible on the narrow road bordered by deep gorges; it was a rout. More than 6,000 soldiers were killed: the entire legion. Grimly, I thought of Quintillus's barb about the "sticks and stones" of the Jews back in Caesarea and suspected his thoughts ran along similar lines.

One misstep by a horse would send both soldier and animal plunging precipitously into a gorge—but the gods smiled on us and our climb into Gibeon was rapid and uneventful. Perhaps the soldiers were eager to get past the site of so much death.

Once we came around a massive formation that Quintillus called the Mount of Olives, the panorama was astounding. Even those soldiers who'd been jesting with one another fell silent as we reached the summit. Although he had made the journey twice before, Quintillus gazed with open reverence at the city gleaming below, nestled amidst a circle of hills.

I dismounted and stood beside my horse in wonder. *Jerusalem truly is a city befitting the gods. No wonder Seneca had wanted to join us.*

Dominating our view was a gleaming, gold-embellished temple that stood at the center of a gigantic white stone platform. Rising upward to the west lay the Upper City, or, as Quintillus called it, *Zion*. The white marble palaces and villas, reminiscent of those in Caesarea, were the homes of the wealthy. Two large, arched passages crossed over from the Upper City to the temple. *This is clearly Herod's work: a majestic home for the*

*gods, soaring heavenward. Herod Antipas, again, I almost feel
sorry for you. What must it be like trying to live up to your father's genius?*

The city was surrounded by a thick gray wall about four
miles in circumference with massive gateways at regular inter-
vals. We crossed through one of these, stopping to exchange
greetings with a publican who seemed pleasantly surprised to
see fellow Romans entering the city.

Quintillus had decided to take the southern route toward
the temple so that we might take the measure of the people we
passed. If there were indeed rebels planning to incite mayhem,
they would most likely live here, in the Lower City.

Jerusalem's splendor faded into drabness as we rode two
by two down its narrow, unpaved streets. The houses were small
and a dull yellowish-brown color, their limestone stained by the
unrelenting sun and wind. Heavily bearded men stood nearly
shoulder to shoulder in front of their houses, watching us, but
there was no sign of women or children. Because of the heavy
facial hair, the men's expressions could not be ascertained. And
when I scanned the crowd, all gazes were downcast, as if searching for secrets in the dust stirred up by our passage.

I wondered which were Sadducees, Pharisees, Scribes,
Samaritans. I further wondered whether any of them really cared
about these arcane distinctions, or were merely foils of Caiaphas
and his lackeys.

I sighed deeply, feeling the weight of these oppressed
people and missing Claudia. The thought of her at this moment
frankly astounded me. This girl—no, she was most definitely a
woman—had wrapped me around her slender fingers! *I love her*,
I realized in wonder. *I love everything about her.*

*Lucius! Focus on the mission at hand. You will have
plenty of time to ponder your good fortune in a wife on the journey back to her.*

It was nearing sundown when we reached the temple

and, true to his word, Caiaphas stood waiting among a cacophony of money-changers and vendors of cattle, doves, and animals for sacrifice, all shouting as loudly as possible.

"Lucius, thank you for coming on such short notice," said the priest—or that is what I assumed he was saying—I could barely hear him above the chaos and commotion.

This is their holy place where they venerate the god who chose them out of all humanity?

The very air felt oppressively heavy. I tried to persuade myself that it was merely weather, but I knew that my feelings had more to do with the contrast between the glory of Jerulasem from a distance and the stark filth of it up close. We had just gotten here, and I could not wait to leave.

I was suddenly happy that I had accepted Seneca's offer to demystify these people for me through his writings. Perhaps his boyhood experience could enlighten me about how I might mediate among the warring factions and zealots residing in this peculiar place.

CHAPTER THIRTY-THREE

"Okay, Antonia, I'll get out if you insist!" Laughing merrily, I grabbed the warm wool peplos she held and wrapped it around me. *Why are my teeth chattering? It's not that cold...*

"Claudia, please do not ever worry us like that again! Zahra and the rest of us have been looking for you everywhere!"

Seeing their agitated expressions, I frowned, confused. "Antonia, why would you be so worried about my brief absence? After Lucius left this morning, I started back to my rooms but turned the wrong way and...well, I had a short swim."

As I spoke, I noticed the position of the sun. When I had come upon the pool, it had been rising. Now it was setting. *How could that be?*

Antonia reacted first. Ignoring what must have seemed an illogical statement, she said, "Come, Claudia, let's get you into dry clothes and find you something to eat."

Zahra regarded me curiously, along with the other serving women whose names I had yet to learn. *Was it possible that I had been in that pool for almost twelve hours?*

Walking through the courtyard toward the east wing of the palace, I held the woolen cloak close and worked my memory back to the period of my swim, and what I had experienced for its duration. I knew that somehow, I had been translocated to Delphi because I'd clearly seen the underground cavern leading to the Oracle. But I could remember nothing after that. There were at least eleven hours I could not account for, and that meant one of two things: Either my concussion had caused some sort of residual brain damage, or...but even as I thought the words, I put them aside. Brain damage would probably have resulted in my drowning, yet here I was—not a bit tired after many hours of exertion. *There is no worldly explanation for this,* I thought. Which left only one possibility: that I had actually traveled somehow to Delphi.

"Claudia!"

Deep in thought, I had walked past the stairs to my suite. As I doubled back and headed toward Antonia with the intention of apologizing, I noted that she was whispering something to Zahra. The Egyptian nodded and smiled in response.

People do not go for a swim for a full day and emerge from it with no memory of the experience. I should be frightened, but...for some reason, I'm not.

In a flash, I did remember something. The shimmering. And not only that but a feeling of the most profound joy intertwined with sorrow and grief. I had been enveloped in something. *Something...not of this world.*

Yet I felt no fear.

CHAPTER THIRTY-FOUR

Lucius Pontius Pilate

The cool air within the palace—there was no other name for the building in which I stood—was a relief from the blazing sun. *Would I ever get accustomed to such heat during winter?*

I had viewed this place from Mount Olive, enjoying the simplicity of the marble fountain and vegetation in the large central courtyard. Unlike the city of Jerusalem, Caiphas's palace was even more beautiful when experienced up close. The rooms I glimpsed as a servant led us up a flight of stairs to the dining area were tastefully furnished, not at all fussy.

We ate while reclining on sofas, which I had always considered "the Roman way," but realized with a start might, in fact, have originated with the Hebrews. Evidently, they had existed far longer than we.

Our talk over the meal was superficial, nothing to disturb the digestion. Caiphas's wife Devorah materialized only once. Clothed in a long robe with a veil over her face, she stepped out from behind a curtain—from the kitchens, I presumed—to ask if there was anything else we required.

A dozen platters sat on the long wooden table, laden with hummus, lamb and beans, olives, figs, and unleavened bread. The fragrance of the lamb was intoxicating. I could not imagine needing anything else, but before I could reply, Annas, Devorah's father, smiled at his daughter and said something to her in Hebrew. Instantly, she faded back behind the beaded, shimmering curtain.

"Thank you, Caiaphas," I said with genuine warmth. "Please extend our gratitude to your wife for such an excellent meal." It was late in the day, and we were tired and hot. I had not expected such delicious food nor the similarities of the cuisine to our own.

Annas sat at the head of the table, gracious but taciturn. Both he and Caiaphas had traded their priestly garments for long robes and turbans. As servants cleared the table and poured tea, I wondered about these two men. Who was really in charge? I knew that Annas had been the Chief Priest before Caiaphas, but had been removed from his position by my predecessor, Valerius. Studying my tea, I considered Annas's replacement: his own son-in-law. The situation was really quite similar to that of our own Caesar, though Roman transfer of leadership took place only upon the death of the Emperor—with no interference from any outside faction.

Watching Annas and Caiaphas dining quietly together, I admired their cleverness. Hands folded in front of his tea, Annas looked into my eyes and said, "Prelate Pilate, Caiaphas and I wish to thank you and your centurion"—a perfunctory nod at Quintillus—"for dining with us. And now there are some delicate matters we wish to discuss with you."

I nodded, ignoring the unspoken request that Quintillus be dismissed.

The silence stretched on, as Annas and Caiaphas looked first at each other, then at me, and finally at Quintillus.

Quintillus's glance at me said, *Shall I leave?*

I responded with a slight shake of my head, *no.*

The gesture did not elude Annas, who started to say something but Caiaphas spoke first. "Lucius, we understand your desire to have your centurion present as a witness to our conversation. So be it."

Annas chimed in, "Prelate, I am aware that my son-in-law gave you very little notice about this journey, and we thank you for your willingness to make haste here, especially so soon after your marriage." For the first time, the man's weathered eyes crinkled into a smile, the only feature clearly visible through his copious facial hair. He looked over at his son-in-law who dutifully smiled and nodded.

Caiaphas peered at Quintillus. "Perhaps I overstated the urgency of this request to you." His bright-green eyes returned to me. "As you can see, our city is peaceful. There are no riots nor is there talk of rebellion."

Then why, by Jove, have you forced us to drag an eighty-man calvary, twenty servants, slaves, horses, and equipment to this place? These men and their machinations...who could figure them? But I willed my expression to remain pleasant, interested. As if I had nothing better to do than make ten-hour treks through the desert.

Patience.

"But there was truth in my request," he continued. "There are some people we are concerned about, and we think you should be as well. We fear they may be enemies of Caesar."

This must be the prophet that Antipas is so anxious about.

I willed myself to meet Caiaphas's gaze rather than look at Quintillus.

"Perhaps Antipas mentioned this man they call John the Baptist?"

I'm confident that Antipas communicated every word of my visit to him in Galilee to you, but apparently, we will never speak frankly.

"Indeed, he did."

After another moment of silence, Caiaphas asked, "Did Herod also tell you of the threats this man is making against him and his wife?"

This time I could not resist a glance at Quintillus, who had happened to be in Rome during the unseemly courtship between the two. Of course, Caiaphas saw the look. I wondered at his use of the word *threat* but said nothing as he described in detail the strange antics of this new prophet, who was drawing more and more people to Jerusalem to be baptized.

CHAPTER THIRTY-FIVE

CAESAREA
Claudia Procula

Antonia, Zahra, and I strolled amidst a chaotic maze of vendors, each shouting about the superior quality of his own produce over that of his neighbor. I stopped to examine some pomegranates, and immediately the man in the adjoining stall called out, "Madame Claudia, come here to see *my* pomegranates. The Governor will much prefer them over Hassan's poor excuse for the fruit of the gods."

"Blasphemy! You dare to call a pomegranate the fruit of the God of Israel?"

Within seconds, the two men stood toe to toe, shouting at each other.

Antonia grabbed my hand while Zahra literally pushed me forward and away from the fracas.

"But…Lucius likes pomegranates! I wanted to get him a few for his—"

"Claudia!" Antonia's exclamation was more a hiss than an approximation of my name. I snapped my head to my left to look at her, but she was already in front of me, pulling me along.

For several minutes, I trotted behind her like the child I still was—and then it hit me that I was a married woman. I dug my heels in and stopped. Mulish, scowling, I looked first at Antonia and then at Zahra and asked spitefully, "Am I confused? I thought *you* were the servants and I the mistress? Is this incorrect?"

Antonia's dark eyes flashed, and Zahra's mouth tightened as she stared fixedly at the dusty street.

The crowd bustled about us heedlessly as we stood there. It was getting late in the afternoon, and the vendors were starting to close up their stalls. In the background, we could hear female voices wheedling lower prices out of the few remaining stands still open.

Regaining her composure, Antonia quietly explained, "Claudia, that vendor. He knew who you were. He called you by name. Did you notice that?"

Now that she had pointed it out, I thought about it. *Antonia's right—that is quite curious. I had never met the man, nor even seen him. I forget I am no longer anonymous but am the wife of Lucius. I should have known to leave the moment he became familiar...*

My defensiveness against my loyal handmaid bled away, and I felt appropriately foolish. As always, she had only my best interests at heart.

"Claudia, people make it their business to know things that might advance their own interests. Lucius is a powerful man in Caesarea and, by association, you wield power as well." She frowned. "I should never have agreed to accompany you here without a detail of soldiers. We will not venture out unprotected again, I can promise you that."

Antonia diplomatically omitted the fact that it had been I who had dismissed the need for guards, insisting that the three of us were quite capable of going out alone. My shame was profound. With a start, a vivid memory from my time in Delphi appeared in my mind. Just four days earlier, the Oracle had been teaching me through questions, precisely as Socrates did with his students. My replies had been flawless, and I'd begun to feel pride in my knowledge...in the ease with which I was able to speak respond.

"What was the most difficult thing?" she'd asked me; and then, "What was the easiest thing?" She'd been quoting Thales.

Glibly, I had replied, "To the first, 'to know thyself.' And to the second, 'to give advice.'"

The Oracle had smiled then, for the first time. In my eagerness to impress her even further, I had continued, "*Gnōthi sauton* most likely has its origin in Egypt, for the inner temple at Luxor is inscribed with, 'Man, know thyself, and you are going to know the gods.'" So focused had I been on flaunting my knowledge that I had not noticed the change in her expression—her obvious disappointment.

"Socrates informed Phaedrus that he 'had no leisure time to explore mythology because he was not yet able, as the Delphic inscription has it, to know myself. So it seems to me ridiculous to investigate irrelevant things.'"

I was still a prideful, ignorant child—and pride born of ignorance was the most dangerous kind.

CHAPTER THIRTY-SIX

CAESAREA
Lucius Pontius Pilate

"Happy birthday, my love. You are seventeen today—an old lady!"

Claudia lay nude in my chambers, looking lovelier even than the day I first saw her. Her long black hair covered the bedclothes, and her eyes sparkled as she watched me enter with her birthday sweet cake. Sabu had learned that the Greeks celebrated birthdays only up until twelve years of age, but I didn't think my bride would mind if I made an exception for her second birthday as a married woman. He had helped me in my efforts by procuring seventeen candles from one of his mysterious sources. He and I had been planning this little surprise ever since I'd returned from my latest series of exhausting, platitudinous meetings with Annas and Caiaphas at their Jerusalem palace. Unfortunately, at least half of the platitudes had been lobbed from my side.

Claudia sat up straight in bed, clapping her hands together like a child. "Oh, husband, you have no idea how very much I have missed birthday cakes. And candles, too!" Her eyes were huge as she gathered her hair together at her neck with one hand, leaned forward, and inhaled deeply in preparation for blowing them out.

"Wait!"

Claudia sat back and exhaled. "What, my love?"

"It's bad fortune to extinguish the candles before receiving your birthday gift." Her eyes danced as I brought my hand from behind my back and held out a scroll. "Your very own copy of the writings of Heraclitus!" I could see her dark eyes filling with tears of surprised joy. I'd chosen well. "Now, Claudia, huge breath. Blow them all out!"

Several hours later, when the cake was mostly crumbs, and we were sated with love and wine, she said, "My gift, Lucius...how did you know?"

I'd consulted Sabu and Antonia, of course, but I didn't feel the need to tell her so. "You are my wife, my heart, and my love," I replied. "Is it not my business to learn what pleases you? What brings you joy?"

It seemed that, even in my transactions with my wife, whom I loved more than life itself, I was becoming a politician.

CHAPTER THIRTY-SEVEN

CAESAREA

Claudia Procula

These peaceful days with Lucius were precious to me—a privilege—and I applied all of my attention joyfully to my husband, who basked in my love, respect, and quietude. Each time he returned from Jerusalem, he was at first distant, almost churlish. He refrained from inviting me to his chambers, although I knew how desperately he must have craved a release.

It took him about twenty-four hours to recover from whatever he'd experienced and come to me: mental exhaustion, perhaps...a type of fatigue far more inimical than the physical kind. From what little I understood of his responsibilities, I imagined that it was the relentless verbal discourse with the priests that poisoned my husband's demeanor.

One of the first things the Oracle had taught me was to be very wary of my natural curiosity—to keep it harnessed. Women, she'd explained, could cause infinite woe to themselves and those they loved in their eagerness to understand the details and machinations of events which occur in life. Consequently, I'd taught myself to swallow my many questions. Over time,

135

they'd stopped appearing in my head.

Lucius had been gone for close to a third of the almost thirty months we had been married, and I was ever conscious of our limited time together. How quickly the moments elapsed; how similar those lost hours, weeks, and months were to the waters of the pool I could never contain in my cupped hands.

I knew that the time we did have was a gift, and was exquisitely aware that the only constant in our lives was flux...change...loss. One would think such knowledge would inspire sorrow and melancholia, that it would dampen the time we had together, but it did not.

The Oracle had asked me if I wished to know the precise time when Lucius and I would be separated finally and forever. She had advised me to take my time before answering because once I knew, I could never "unknow."

I'd realized at that moment, that she was giving me an opportunity to hold back my curiosity. It had taken just a few minutes to understand that the weight of the knowledge she'd offered me would crush me. And my beloved. I'd refused the knowledge, with boundless gratitude for the insight I'd gained in considering it.

"CLAUDIA, WAKE UP!!!"

I opened my eyes, still dazed from a dream, to find Lucius leaning over me anxiously.

"You were shouting my name, Claudia...begging me to have nothing to do with 'that righteous man!' Who on earth were you dreaming about?"

I stared at my husband, then blinked hard to clear my mind.

But we've been together for just four years. Not yet, please. Not yet!

"Nobody, my love. I was just having a nightmare—a silly dream—that's all." I smiled at my husband as convincingly as I could, abruptly aware that some kind of countdown had begun. Lucius had so many worries—I had no desire to add to them. But as I watched him relax in relief, I realized that for the first time, I had seen the face of the man in my dreams.

Did that mean we had only days or weeks together?

CHAPTER THIRTY-EIGHT

CAESAREA

Lucius Pontius Pilate

The fault for the riot that ended the lives of four Hebrew boys lay squarely at my feet. It was due to that most banal of all vices: *hubris*, the Greek word for pride I had learned as a boy. *Hubris* was the downfall of better men than I. Just as the heroes in the ancient Greek tragedies had done, I turned a blind eye to my own Cassandra.

The truth was, I was fed up with the tedium of my *officium*. When I mentally recited Cicero's counsel, the words turned to ashes in my mind. *There are, therefore, instances of civic courage that are not inferior to the courage of the soldier. Indeed, civic service calls for even greater energy and even greater devotion.*

This was not devotion or courage but rather a perverted obeisance.

My efforts to reassure myself that I had had a reasonable—even noble—reason for doing what I did…that it had been out of reverence for Tiberius and his role as Emperor...these were lies. In reality, I had been so discontented with the unending treks to Jerusalem that I had decided to do anything I could think of to end the dreadful monotony.

After almost four years of responding to the seemingly whimsical directives of Annas and Caiaphas by making the long trek to Jerusalem, I'd decided to exhibit some initiative. Of course, I'd come up with justifications for my actions, and a most reasonable argument in my defense.

Every Caesar, including Sulla, was stamped on one of the coins used for everyday commerce throughout the Roman Empire. One of my first major actions upon arrival in Caesarea had been a risky financial maneuver spurred by the ever-expanding debt of the Empire. Coins had been in very short supply for a host of reasons, and if the situation continued, the people would be incapable of paying their taxes. In response, I reopened the mintage that my predecessor Valerius had closed and, upon obtaining the Emperor's approval to do so, stamped out hundreds of thousands of new coins—but with a two percent reduction in their gold and silver content. (This was a necessary stricture based on the severely strained finances of Rome, and I knew Tiberius would look kindly upon it.)

Each coin—excepting the As and Dupondius—bore an image of Tiberius. The two exceptions depicted Caesar Augustus. If "graven images" were acceptable on the currency trafficked by the competing money-lenders outside of their so-called sacred temple in Jerusalem, why, then, would the images on my troops' military standards cause the Jews any consternation? Such had been the justification for my decision.

Both Seneca and Cicero had advised that the sole method for controlling these people was pure oppression. Give them no leeway. I still believed a bit more finesse was called for...until that dreadful day.

I had studied the extensive materials sent by Seneca for close to a year, and, in spite of the aggressive stance they seemed to support, I had concluded that I must be patient; must proceed in a manner wholly different from that of Valerius. I would heed the counsel of Quintillus and behave as I had done when I was Tribune of the greatest army in the world. I would be the man I had always been: self-controlled, never giving in to impulse or willfulness. I would remain the master of inferior emotions such as anger, pride, passion, and revenge.

That I had been able to maintain such a standard for as long as I did was due almost entirely to Claudia. Ever since our wedding, I'd known that Seneca evoked a strong reaction in my wife. She'd exhibited the self-possession of Quintillus, but a flash in her eyes had communicated her distrust. Her concerns seemed to be amplified when she saw me studying his writings. I only wish I'd heeded her more fully.

Seneca quoted Cicero liberally as evidence for his claim that the animosity of Romans toward Hebrews was not only justified but a linchpin of our responsibility as citizens. That Cicero considered Jews an enemy of the Empire, I recalled from my boyhood studies of *Pro Flacco*. Only recently did I stop to consider the facts of that famous trial, and the strange similarities between the Roman soldier Flaccus and me.

A former legionary soldier of Rome, Flaccus was appointed Prelate of Asia by Caesar, only to be accused of stealing tax money intended for Rome. In defense of Flaccus, Cicero pointed to the man's bravery in battle and rapid rise through the ranks as proof of his impeccable character. The famed lawyer then proceeded to vitiate the testimony of the witnesses for the prosecution by emphasizing the inherent untrustworthiness and dishonesty of the Jewish peoples. Ultimately, Cicero succeeded in persuading the jurors of his client's innocence by mounting an *ad hominem* attack on the Jews while invoking the bravery of Flaccus in battle.

The fact that Seneca had written at length about the case—and had then bestowed these writings on me as "necessary reading"—was no accident. Clearly, he'd intended to highlight what he saw as conspicuous similarities between a long-dead fellow soldier and me. I did feel an eerie sense of camaraderie with the man. Even before I was accused of extorting the Jerusalem temple funds, Flaccus felt like a brother-in-arms.

Very conveniently, I had turned a deaf ear to the precedent set by my predecessors, the warnings of Quintillus, and my own training against just this kind of emotional decision—which was really more of a *reaction* than a *choice*.

Rome had authorized the addition of a new legion to Judea. Caiaphas and Annas's anxieties about the new Jerusalem prophets were such that they were constantly asking for more soldiers. In fact, Caiaphas had made it clear that he wanted me in Jerusalem at all times.

In appreciation for Tiberius's granting of my request, I decided to personally lead the First Cohort of 800 on a ritual tour of Caesarea before we began the arduous trek to Jerusalem. In attempts to mollify Caiaphas, Quintillus, his lead centurion Longinus, and Gracian had stayed in Jerusalem at my command. Had Quintillus been with me, would I have done it? Held aloft the military standard with the Caesar Tiberius's image and golden eagle for all the Caesarean citizens to see?

Had I known that the reaction would be an extreme one?

Yes, I had to admit it; I'd known these people would be incensed—perhaps even enough so that they'd pry Caiaphas out of his palace and dispatch him from Jerusalem, forcing him to come to me for once.

But never did I envision the virulence of the riots in the streets, nor the bloodthirstiness of the mostly foreign, untrained troops. Foolishly, I had left them to return to the palace to say my goodbyes to Claudia before leaving for Jerusalem.

As I'd left, I'd seen a group of young Hebrews taunting

a group of dismounted soldiers. Utter fool that I was, my exact thought had been, "Good, this will precipitate some bloodshed—enough for Caiaphas to take note."

I did not intend, nor did I foresee, the deaths that would follow when three of my soldiers got into a fight with four youths armed only with stones.

CHAPTER THIRTY-NINE

CAESAREA
Claudia Procula

I climbed out of the pool, shivering. It was late in the afternoon, and there was a chill in the air. Blindly groping for my shawl, I realized that I had once again been submerged for many hours. My mind and heart were filled with portent, and I knew our time was growing short.

Once again, the Oracle had asked if I wanted to know just how much time Lucius and I had remaining. I wept at her question because I already knew the answer—not the precise date, of course, but the imminence and inevitability. The mere fact that she had asked again, coupled with the knowledge that she and I would meet no more, undid me.

I did not notice his hand until it was on me, wrapping the wool peplos securely around me. "Claudia, you are freezing to death," he whispered. "Come here, my love, and warm your hands at the fire."

Blinking rapidly, trying to clear my vision of pool water and tears, I stared at my husband.

Why is he here? He never comes to the pool...Something

awful must have happened.

I desperately wanted to ask him why he looked so stricken, but I held my tongue. My mind was spinning, searching for an explanation for my love's odd behavior and demeanor. I had seen Lucius studying those hateful writings from Seneca. I had observed his growing frustration with the High Priests in Jerusalem and their concocted "matters of great urgency." Our time together no longer constituted an oasis for my husband, as he found it increasingly difficult to shuck off the cares of his office. Only rarely could Lucius access the peace of mind that he had enjoyed in our early days together.

Looking deeply into his eyes, I could see so much. He had made some kind of decision, and people had died as a consequence. There were sorrow, regret, and dread suffusing the soul of the man I loved.

CHAPTER FORTY

CAESAREA
Lucius Pontius Pilate

"We have no graven image before the Lord of Abraham, of Elijah, of Moses. The Lord, Our God, is Holy. You are blaspheming His Name!" Thus shouted fourteen-year-old Joshua, sixteen-year-old Eli, sixteen-year-old Isaiah, and seventeen-year-old David, raising their heads in defiance and exposing their young and tender throats to my soldiers.

It took but three of my men to spear all four swiftly through their hearts. That the legionnaires were not Roman soldiers but Idumeans wearing the uniform of the Empire was but the barest consolation. Two of the dead Hebrew boys were the only sons of a widow; the others were aspiring rabbis in residence at the temple. Before I left for Jerusalem, I was determined to go alone to the home of the widow to express my sorrow and offer financial assistance.

It took a while for Sabu to determine where the woman lived, but he managed it. As he walked with me down the steps and through the courtyards of the palace, he expressed his dim view of my proceeding down the street unaccompanied at midday and visiting the home of the bereaved mother. I listened politely but remained resolute.

I could not have mistaken the house had I been blind; the wailing and lamentation could be heard throughout the neighborhood. I took a deep breath as I approached, suddenly feeling very exposed.

More than fifty people had gathered in the modest courtyard. Sabu had predicted as much: "These families extend to second, third, and fourth cousins, aunts and uncles," he'd explained. "There will be a large crowd of all ages. The women will all be wearing black. The men will want nothing less than your head in revenge for the death of these boys."

My heart beat faster as, one by one, the mourners saw and recognized me and the clamor subsided.

As I stood in the middle of the courtyard, completely surrounded by Jews, the silence was profound. I scanned the crowd and noticed a woman near the entrance to the small home. Behind her was a small group of women clad in black.

Into the stunned silence, I asked, "Is there anyone here who speaks Greek?"

An elderly man in what looked like the garb of a rabbi quietly replied, "Yes. I do."

He must have known the two boys who'd been studying at the temple.

"Thank you, Rabbi. I am Lucius Pontius Pilate. I have come to extend my sincere apology and express my deep remorse at the deaths of Joshua, Eli, Isaiah, and David."

The boys' names instigated a resurgence of the mournful wailing.

The rabbi raised his hand to the crowd, spoke a few words, and silence once again blanketed the courtyard. He continued speaking to them quietly in Hebrew. He was translating what I'd said.

Suddenly, two men who looked to be about my age

shoved their way forward through the crowd—relatives of the dead boys, perhaps. Their expressions were malevolent, and their hands held stones. Big ones.

The rabbi spoke again, quietly. The men ignored him and moved closer to me. This time, the rabbi shouted. He glared. Finally, reluctantly, they dropped the stones and receded back into the crowd, their heads dropped low.

The rabbi looked at me. "Continue," he said.

"I cannot undo the savage acts of my soldiers," I said, "but I would like, at the very least, to offer recompense to the survivors of the smitten youths. I want to assure the widow who lost her sons that she will have no financial worries for the rest of her life. And I would like to make a donation to your temple in the names of Isaiah and David."

The strident, angry voices that then rose above mine were female. Before I could determine the source of the cries, the rabbi again broke in, cutting them off.

Turning to me, he said, "Sir, I recognize that you did not need to come here, to risk appearing here among us alone. Nor did you need to offer restitution. You did these things of your own free will, and I, for one, am grateful." With that, he bowed to me. And, for the first time since the horrible act had taken place, I hoped that perhaps we might restore peace after all. Perhaps I could be granted *expiatio*—what the Jews would call *atonement*. I felt almost clean, and profound gratitude to this rabbi.

CHAPTER FORTY-ONE

Lucius Pontius Pilate

"I will never forgive myself for leaving these men without adequate leadership in the midst of a riot created by my actions," I said frankly to Caiaphas.

"Have the men responsible been executed?"

Word traveled fast in Judea. By the time I'd arrived, the High Priests had been informed of the riot and its deadly consequences, and of my visit to the home of the bereaved. I was exactly where Caiaphas wanted me. He had the desired additional legion of troops, minus the hapless Idumeans who had been responsible for the killing. Those four soldiers could thank Quintillus for their lives. And I had agreed to remain in Jerusalem throughout the first phase of construction of the new aqueduct. It would take at least two months, probably closer to six.

Truth be told, I was astounded that my heedlessness had not cost me my job. Miraculously, I remained Prefect, but for how long, I did not know. When my message detailing the incident had arrived in Rome, Tiberius might have acted in a number of ways—from conferring a commendation upon me to taking

148

away my position, to ending my life. If Sejanus had had any influence, I'm sure it would have been the last. But, as it happened, Tiberius had been extravagant with his praise when I reopened the Caesarea mintage, and that action had surely helped determine my fate. It was yet to be seen whether my plan for the Jerusalem aqueduct would be perceived as recklessly extravagant or brilliant.

Caiaphas revealed nothing as he awaited my response to his question about the soldiers' fate, but his eyes were soft. Quintillus and I were seated in our usual places at the table in his courtyard, across from him and his father-in-law. I looked to my right where my friend sat quietly, then returned my gaze to Caiaphas. "Quintillus was quite right in insisting that their lives be spared," I finally replied. "The fault was wholly my own."

Both sets of heavy white eyebrows shot up. Caiaphas opened his mouth to speak, but Annas cut him off. "Please tell us about the aqueduct, Lucius. You say you would start at Solomon's Pool near Bethlehem? And build out over thirty-five kilometers to the Temple?"

His eyes were shining.

CHAPTER FORTY-TWO

CAESAREA
Claudia Procula

Worried that there might be attempts on my life in retribution for the deaths of the boys, Lucius had sent Gracian and a few other legionnaires back from Jerusalem. Until I saw the eight soldiers enter the courtyard, I had not thought I was concerned, but when they arrived, I flew down the staircase to greet them.

Gracian was in the lead, and he smiled broadly upon seeing me—but I noted that he looked quite tired.

"How good to see you, Gracian!" I said, extending my hand to the soldier who had saved my life. "May we fix you a light supper?" Sabu, Antonia, and Zahra were right behind me. Of course, they had heard about the riots and deaths and, like me, were relieved to see the eight-strong warriors.

As he reached the top of the stairs, Gracian looked back at his men and said, "What is your pleasure, men? We rode hard and well. Seven hours from Jerusalem to Caesarea might warrant a prize."

Although it was after nine in the evening, it was not yet twilight—one of June's many delights. I hoped the men would accept my invitation to dine, as I had many questions for Gracian, who felt like a brother to me after all we'd been through.

After a moment, one of the men spoke up for the group. "To be sure, Gracian, we've not had anything to eat since sunrise...but..." He hesitated, looking at Sabu's spotless long white robe. "...what about the horses?"

Sabu smiled. "Not to worry, sir. I have two men attending to them now. They will be brushed down, given food and water, and settled into the palace stalls."

Without waiting for further discussion, the young servant rubbed his hands together and said: "Madame Claudia, please show these gentlemen to the dining room while we prepare a light supper."

Once we'd settled around the capacious table, upon which had been spread a light repast consisting of fragrant couscous, assorted grilled meats, and cheeses. Gracian said, "I wish I could tell you how Lucius is, Claudia, but I did not see him. As soon as he arrived in Jerusalem last night, he went to the palace of Caiaphas and Annas. He stopped at the barracks only momentarily to retrieve Quintillus and tell us to leave for Caesarea in the morning."

I nodded, disappointed.

"Lucius will be there for a while, I fear. That is one reason he sent us here." Gracian studied me. "You look well, Claudia. It has been..." He stopped to calculate.

"Four years in just four months," I interjected.

"It seems so much longer!"

We shared a laugh at the vagaries of time and at our similar lines of thought.

Placing my hand on his scarlet-uniform-clad arm, I said, "Eat, please, my friend. These lamb kabobs are one of Sabu's finest preparations. He will be hurt if we don't clean our plates."

The food was indeed delicious. Until the soldier spoke

about the last time he had eaten, I hadn't realized how hungry I was myself—having not eaten since the previous evening. The lamb was perfectly cooked, as always.

Lucius will be gone for a while.

That normally meant a couple of months, at least.

Thank you, husband, for assuring my safety when you have so very much on your mind.

Sabu hovered over me. "Are you feeling alright, Madame? Half your plate remains."

"I am feeling wonderful, Sabu….Just taking my time enjoying the meal you have so deftly prepared, and grateful that our Roman friends have joined us."

CHAPTER FORTY-THREE

BETHLEHEM
Lucius Pontius Pilate

Leaning on my pick, I squinted into the sun and used the tunic wrapped around my now very lean waist to wipe away some of the sweat dripping into my eyes. Then I looked around in vain for a clean one, since I wore only a loincloth. A rider was approaching rapidly, and I felt it unseemly to be half-dressed like a slave—even though I was working every bit as hard as one. Perceiving my dilemma, Benignus laughed and tossed over his snow-white tunic. I'd been working beside him for nearly three months.

"We've broken through to the bridge!" Jacobus proclaimed as he leapt from his horse and raced toward me, both hands in the air. "You have done it, sir! In just a few days, they will have so much water at the temple that the animals will drown before the priests have a chance to sacrifice them!"

I have done nothing. Our success is due to the sheer genius of Roman engineers like you, Jacobus. But by Jove, I have certainly offered my body, strength, and will—as have my entire legion—to do the impossible.

We had been digging for so many twelve-hour days in a row that I had lost track of anything but the work. It felt wonderful. Overwhelmed with awe and gratitude, I could say nothing to Jacobus; I mutely accepted the rib-crushing embrace of the tall young soldier who had made it all happen.

Within seconds, word swept through our crew of one hundred soldiers, and the sound of axes, picks, and other tools dropping to the ground mingled with the rousing cheers of the men. I stood watching the celebration and thought back over our days and weeks of camaraderie. The grueling physical exertion had melded us into a genuine brotherhood, and I had loved every moment of it—even those first couple of weeks when my body was a study in pain. I offered silent thanks that, against the advice of Quintillus, I had come up here to join the effort—leaving him in charge—rather than staying in Jerusalem and growing softer and paler.

I reflected on how it had all started...about how Fortuna had smiled on me once again...impelling me to stop and *listen* to this annoying young Roman soldier, Jacobus.

My fervor to do something significant for these people had only grown stronger on the journey back to Jerusalem after the riots and ensuing tragedy. This time, when I stopped the cavalry for the customary rest at the summit before heading down into the city, I viewed the temple with new eyes.

Whereas before, it had appeared as a stunning monument to Herod's architectural genius, I now regarded it with something akin to reverence. Seen from on high, the Jerusalem temple looked like a city, its walls over seventy meters high and its sanctuary rising one hundred meters more. With the rays of the setting sun illuminating the gold filigree atop the sanctuary, it looked ethereal.

The insistent shouts of the boys shortly before they met their ends echoed in my mind as I studied the splendor of this monument sacred to the Jews: *We have no graven image before*

*the Lord of Abraham, of Elijah, of Moses. The Lord, our God, is
holy. You are blaspheming His name!*

Like everyone who passed through the city, I knew that
the Gihon Spring was woefully inadequate for the Jews' animal
sacrifices. On feast days, the odor of the blood of thousands of
animals remained for days. Of course, I had never been inside
the sanctuary, but where once I had joined my soldiers in heck-
ling the temple guards as they tried to clean up the dried and
stinking residue, I now felt sorrow for the desecration of their
most holy edifice. Not just animal blood had been shed for this
unshakeable faith of theirs.

The solution to their problem was simple—and one that
I could provide. Water. We would build an aqueduct, just as we
had done throughout all of the lands of the Empire.

Quintillus had remained silent throughout the three-hour
meeting with the Priests to present the idea, but I had caught him
looking at me with an expression I knew well. *Lucius, is this un-
dertaking a good idea—and is it even possible?*

Walking back to the barracks, I'd remained engrossed
in the challenge of it all, pondering so many questions that it
had taken me a moment to notice Jacobus when he approached.

"Sir, I hear we are going to build an aqueduct for the
temple."

I stared at the tall young man, a Roman, who had interrupted my train of thought. "Who are you?" I snapped.

I looked at Quintillus, but he merely shrugged.

The smile on the young face faded and his cheeks
flushed, but he stood his ground. "Sir, I am Jacobus. I was reas-
signed to you from Syria, where we just completed a buildout of
an aqueduct extending almost fifteen kilometers. I arrived when
you did, just a few hours ago."

Still not appreciating who stood before me, I commented
dryly, "I see the legion pipeline travels fast, treating even insane
rumors as truth. Jacobus...the truth is, we don't even know if

such a thing is possible."

The man's smile returned and widened into a grin. "Oh but it is, sir! We can do this. In fact, I believe there has previously been an aqueduct here—in fact, I am confident of it."

I looked over at Quintillus once more, and he shook his head in amazement. We both proceeded to listen as Jacobus explained that the bridge we had crossed over on our way to the temple had once served as an aqueduct. He lost me as he explained the engineering behind a *sealed siphon system*, which, he insisted, was the only thing that would have warranted the careful composition of concrete, paste, and sealer that composed that bridge.

"There's a water source here, sir. Somewhere within twenty-five kilometers of the city."

Just two days later we found the source, just as Jacobus had predicted we would. Just south of Bethlehem were three large, rectangular pools—reservoirs. The largest of the three was at least fifty feet deep. Jacobus excitedly pointed out the stone pipe segments, evidence of an aqueduct that had functioned centuries before. As he explained it, the sealed siphon system operated on the principle of gravity—water flows downhill. The whole concept struck me as simple and brilliant.

CHAPTER FORTY-FOUR

JERUSALEM
Lucius Pontius Pilate

Caiaphas's scribbled message insisting upon my return after just a few days at home with Claudia had been clever and commanding:

> *Herod has arrested the Baptizer. A Galilean they are calling the Messiah is drawing people from all over Judea and Galilee. The people claim he has raised the dead. Some are referring to this man as King of Israel. This prophet is dangerous. He is teaching my people that there is a man superior to Caesar.*

There was no way I could ignore the summons. Caiaphas's claim that there were those insisting that Caesar was not a god indicated treason.

This time, just six soldiers made the trek with Quintillus and me, to join the legion of 6000 men of various backgrounds I had positioned there permanently a year earlier—a move that had merited appreciation from Annas and Caiaphas at the time.

157

We made it to Jerusalem in just under eight hours—a record of sorts. I had joked to Quintillus along the way that our horses were beginning to know the treacherous route so well that they could traverse it blindfolded.

As we entered the city, we noted the change in the character of the place. What we were faced with was a far cry from the suppressed hostility with which we had been confronted upon our first visit. True, there were groups of men loitering outside their homes as before, but their conversations seemed vibrant. Many of them were so engrossed in chatter that they barely noted us as we passed on the way to the palace.

Initially, I did not understand why the two high priests were so troubled by the man they described, this *Jesus of Nazareth*. I asked Quintillus to attend some of his orations, and after listening to three of them, my trusted colleague returned to tell me that this "prophet" spoke only of love, peace, and forgiveness. If rebellion against Rome lay in his heart, he betrayed none of it. In fact, when someone in the crowd asked him a direct question about Rome, the man replied, "Render unto Caesar the things that are Caesar's and to God, the things that are God's."

A chill coursed down my spine as I listened to Quintillus and noted his genuine respect—admiration, even—for this *Jesus*. He told me of the thousands who'd gathered on a hilltop and listened for hours while the new prophet spoke not of rules, sacrifices, or restrictions, but of the love of his father for each one of them. *Was the man really claiming to be the son of the Hebrew God?*

As we stood on the veranda overlooking the old city, Quintillus remained so intent on relating his impressions of Jesus that he did not at first notice my reaction. When our gazes finally locked, our thoughts seemed to merge. *They cannot let this man continue to influence his people. The power of the High Priests resides in the fact that this religion of theirs encompasses many warring factions governed by some 613 laws—laws that require*

the likes of Annas and Caiaphas to interpret them. This constant,
fractious squabbling among competing factions is critical if Ca-
iaphas and his father-in-law are to maintain control. And then
there's the money...on feast days, the income generated for the
Priests had to be a staggering sum.

Miraculously in unison, Quintillus and I declared, "He
is uniting them!" We both understood that if these Scribes, Pharisees, and Sadducees ceased their internecine battles, they might
well unite against a common enemy.

After several days of meetings with Caiaphas and
Annas, their anxiety had diminished enough that Quintillus and
I began to make preparations for our return home. Then we
learned that the fool Herod Antipas had murdered the man they
called John the Baptist. Drunk at some feast, he had ordered the
prophet's beheading.

My heart sank as dreams of Caesarea, and my life with
Claudia faded into an indefinite future.

Strangely, the time I'd been spending with the two High
Priests had changed my attitude toward them. Instead of feeling
angry and resentful at the time and energy they consumed, I
began to sense our commonalities. To be sure, Caiaphas and I
were not friends—not even allies in any real sense. I disliked his
constant dissembling, the verbal duels, and manipulation that
were projections of his nature. But I recognized him as a man
not totally dissimilar from me. He had a lofty job, one that I was
confident he'd worked hard to attain. Certainly, learning the in-
tricacies of Mosaic law had not come easily. That Annas was his
father-in-law had surely helped him attain his position, and he
had Annas's counsel to help him keep it. But I could not deny
the fact that he and I faced similar challenges of statesmanship.

Had Augustus Caesar still been Emperor of the Roman
Empire, Lucius Pontius Pilate would not be Prelate of Judea. Almost certainly, in fact, I would be dead—if not as a consequence
of the riots in Caesarea, then for my decision to rebuild a thirty-

seven-kilometer aqueduct without advance permission from Rome. Tiberius and I had fought together on many a blood-soaked field in Germania, and for that reason alone, he had approved the bold and costly project. We were close to completing it when formal approval finally arrived.

CHAPTER FORTY-FIVE

CAESAREA

Claudia Procula

"Please, Claudia, come with me. I've already asked Gracian if he or one of his soldiers might accompany us."

I stared at Antonia. The usually unflappable woman was so excited that she could not stand still. She was literally bouncing on her feet.

Holding my stare, she said, "They call him a prophet! He's staying for just a few more hours now that the wedding is over."

"Where do we need to go to see this miraculous individual?" I asked, suppressing a smile at her enthusiasm.

"The house of my friend, Esther," she replied. "It was at her daughter's wedding that he turned water into wine!"

Turned water into wine? And so it begins.

Antonia was too agitated to notice the color drain from my face or the shudder that coursed through my body. As she departed my suite, she called out over her shoulder, "Esther's home is near the harbor so I will bring your woolen peplos against the chill. We'll need to leave very soon so we can hear him speak. I imagine there will be a huge crowd!"

A wrong turn at the harbor made us a bit late, but as we came around a bend, Gracian pointed out the large crowd gathered at a house to our southwest. It was ten more minutes before we arrived and by then the crowd had swelled even further. I was surprised to see so many women—and such a diverse gathering. These were not just Hebrews and Samarians, but Greeks, Syrians, and others whose dress and demeanor were unfamiliar to me. They seemed to be from all walks of life, too: highborn next to servant and even slave.

Although we stood at the periphery, I could hear the prophet clearly.

"If any man would come after me, let him deny himself and take up his cross and follow me. For whoever would save his life would lose it, and whoever loses his life for my sake gains it. For what does it profit a man to gain the whole world and lose his life? For whoever is ashamed of me and of my words in this adulterous and sinful generation, of him will the son of man also be ashamed when he comes in the glory of his Father with the holy angels."

What language is he speaking? It is neither Greek nor Latin, and I speak only those two tongues—and yet I understand his words.

It was not just that we all understood what he said; it was the words themselves that made the speech unlike any other. It was full of contradictions and paradox, and yet it made blinding sense. And the *way* he spoke…the man never shouted nor attempted to persuade; he simply spoke with quiet prerogative and portent. The crowd stood in rapt silence as if being fed by his oration.

I turned to see if I could get the attention of Antonia or Gracian, but both were focused single-mindedly on the speaker before us, nodding periodically in clear understanding. As I looked around, I saw Syrians, Idumeans, even Cappadocians pressed in on one another without incident. All were still. All were transfixed.

How can this be?

A group of men who looked like Greeks carried a pallet on which lay an immobile man through the crowd toward the speaker. The four of them struggled under the dead weight; the unfortunate man must have been a paralytic. The crowd parted to let them through until finally, they lay the litter at the feet of the prophet. I could not hear what the holy man said next, but after just a minute or two, the man on the pallet stretched, sat up, then stood and walked. A collective gasp arose from the crowd, and I can't deny I participated in it.

The row of men in front of us began to talk among themselves. "What is this?" one murmured. "He speaks with authority and casts out demons," said another. "He can heal the lame!"

Antonia nodded toward the men and whispered, "They are scribes from the temple."

I wondered how she knew this until I looked over at her friend, who stood smiling and nodding at the words of the prophet. *She knows him personally,* I realized. *Of course, she would have explained a great deal about him and their religion to Antonia.*

I looked again at the scribes and noticed the phylacteries attached to their right arms. Once, at the market, Antonia had pointed out the strange objects, along with the ten fringes on the stoles worn by all of the men.

The men were right in their remarks about the prophet—he did speak with an authority that could only come from certainty and inner wisdom.

The holy man was moving now, walking quickly and gracefully through the crowd. When I had a clear view of him, I could see that he was tall—about Lucius's height—with long chestnut-colored hair. Unlike most men of his tradition, he wore no beard. A small group of his followers encircled him as if to protect him from the crowd. Suddenly, I became aware of a young mother pushing her way through the crowd, holding her fretting baby aloft. She worked her way toward the prophet until she stood squarely in front of him, barring his way.

His followers, annoyed at the interruption, shouted, "Madame, let him pass!"

But, with a small gesture of his hand, he stopped their tongues and approached the woman. He gently took the screaming child into his arms and smiled down at it with pure, radiant love. The baby instantly stopped crying and lay peacefully in his arms.

"Truly, I say unto you, unless you turn and become like children, you will never enter the kingdom of heaven," he said to the crowd. "Whoever humbles himself like this child, he is greatest in the kingdom of heaven."

The baby reached up to tug at his lower lip, smiling and gurgling. The prophet took the tiny hand in his and kissed it.

"Whoever receives one such child in my name, receives me; but whoever causes one of these little ones who believe in me to sin, it would be better for him to have a great millstone fastened round his neck and to be drowned in the depth of the sea."

I had never seen or heard the like. Quite clearly, neither had anyone else gathered there, for, after the man stopped talking, there was a long moment of pure silence, broken only by the happy gurgling of the baby in his arms.

CHAPTER FORTY-SIX

It has been several months since I went to hear the man who is called Jesus. The name, Antonia tells me, means *savior.* I've spent much of my time since then deepening my understanding of Plato's *Symposium* and the writings of Heraclitus, the philosopher who first wrote of *logos* and of *absolutes.* I felt it worthwhile to memorize passages from Heraclitus because his words describe the currents of my life so aptly.

> *All things come out of the One and the One out of all things...I see nothing but Becoming. Be not deceived! It is the fault of your limited outlook and not the fault of the essence of things if you believe that you see firm land anywhere in the ocean of Becoming and Passing. You need names for things, just as if they had a rigid permanence, but the very river in which you bathe a second time is no longer the same one which you entered before...*

Contradiction and paradox, but I know the words are

true. Even before my time with the Oracle, I understood that things were not what they seemed; that much of what we believed was a result of the "inconvenience" of the truth, and of our need to exalt ourselves and our powers.

The words of Heraclitus feel as if they could have been spoken by the man called Jesus...if he was indeed, the personification of *logos*, perhaps they were. But, where Plato and Heraclitus wrote of *logos* as a kind of anonymous entity, Jesus represents himself as the *son of man*. A most curious expression, one that subtly extends an invitation, not just to the Jewish people but to all.

He has spoken of his *father*...as if he has a personal relationship with this entity. This reminds me of Sabina with her Greek gods and goddesses. And yet, somehow, his God is not like Athena or even Apollo at all. Sabina has indicated that she thinks of Athena as someone with whom she shares human intimacy.

Antonia traveled to Tyre and, several weeks later, to Capernaum to hear him speak. She and Esther, the mother of the girl with the miraculous wine, have become good friends. Antonia invited me to join her on each journey and seemed unsurprised—if a bit disappointed—at my refusal to accompany her. I have told her nothing of my dreams, but I suspect she has heard me, as Lucius has, calling out in my sleep.

Lucius has been in Jerusalem for most of the past eight months. As difficult as that is for both of us, I understand that it is for the best because soon I will be without him altogether and I must prepare myself for this on two levels.

First and primarily, I must resist the temptation to allow my fears to bleed into the finite hours remaining to us. Both my studies and my observations of the reality of life have impressed on me the need—indeed, the imperative—to plumb joy from each moment; that includes those filled mostly with grief and sorrow. They are curious things, these emotions of joy and sorrow—allies of a sort. Even during moments of intense, ecstatic joy, sorrow remains present, waiting in the shadows.

My salutary effect upon Lucius is profound, I know, but only if I keep my passions reined in. Of course, I am not speaking here about the sublime passion of lovemaking, where there need be no control whatsoever. In the congress of man and wife, it is only in the absence of restraint that sublime heights can be reached. What I speak of when I refer to reining myself in is the lower passion of selfishness, incited by curiosity and fear. These feelings must be manacled. I must, for example, resist the urge to shout at my husband, *Why don't you act as I would? How can you not see the consequences that image of Tiberius will have upon the Hebrews? Why don't you ask for my opinion?*

Believe me when I say that I knew Seneca's influence on Lucius would cause him devastation. I desired with all my heart to tell him so—to warn him that ingesting such hateful things about the people he was sent to govern could only incite fear and enmity in the Hebrews. What held me back from speaking out was the many hours I'd spent with the Oracle, when she impressed upon me the mysteries of conjugal love and the strange paradox that accompanies it... the inability to protect the love of my heart from himself. My wisdom could not be conferred to another, even Lucius.

I now understand that the "fable" told to Socrates was less an allegory than a parable, much like those that Jesus tells. Their meanings are comprehensible only to those with ears to hear and eyes to see: those who hunger for truth, and who apprehend that this reality we see in front of us is but a shadow of the real thing.

Not infrequently, I think back on myself as that thirteen-year-old child who arrogantly claimed to understand the words of Aristophanes on love in Plato's *Symposium*. Uncle Adrian's response seems not just poignant but painful in retrospect. Did he speak this way because he and Aunt Sabina were soul mates?

Or, were they not? Either condition would warrant his provocative statement:

> *Child, that allegory about the origin of humanity that Aristophanes tells, when it is his turn to speak, has ignited controversy ever since Plato first published* The Symposium. *Was Aristophanes jesting, as in one of his comedies? Or was that complicated story about the original humans being split in half and forever searching for the lost other half of themselves—the soulmate—both promise and portent for human lovers until the end of time?*

That concept of *soulmate*, that missing half of ourselves, is no longer philosophy. In those first three days of my marriage, the union with Lucius altered the entire fabric of my being. In those seventy-two hours, I became whole. An emptiness hitherto unknown to me was filled, creating a literal *fusion* that is unrepeatable.

Uncle's haunting words of promise and portent describe precisely the paradox of lovers. The union elevates us to heights known only by the gods, where, we participate in the wordless language of the divine—of wisdom. Nothing is lacking; all is sufficient. Alas, it is a state incompatible with real life.

Once Lucius left to carry out his responsibilities and I began my schooling at Delphi, the two of us could never return to that state we knew in those blissful days. The gates were forever shut.

When a man and a woman—even true soulmates—return to their separate selves and the daily routines of life, they come to oppose each other. I could sense what was in the mind and heart of my husband as he faced the increasingly powerful forces of his destiny, but I could not confer my wisdom upon him. If I were to attempt to do so, I would be doing battle with fate.

When forced back into the coarse imprecision of spoken communication, we humans inhabit a dangerous territory—one riddled with the explosive landmines called words. Man and woman become alien to each other because, by nature, we are antipodal. Lucius became as much a stranger to me as any man on earth. I could no more understand him or his motives than the mysteries of this man called Jesus.

Until afterward, that is. When it was too late.

It was our fate that Lucius and I would remain essentially alone, despite the deep love we shared.

The second way in which I must prepare myself for Lucius's absence is no less important than the first. I must internalize the fundamental teaching of the Oracle when, on frequent occasions, she dropped her hands into the Castalian Spring and wriggled her fingers in the cold and crystal-clear water. She frowned as she made a fist and tried to collect the water in her hands—to no avail—then nodded at me to do the same. But of course, I could not hold on to the water any more than she could. This, she repeated over and over during those first mystical days in Delphi. At the time, I did not understand this repetition of actions that seemed to make no sense. Over and over I would ask her to explain.

She would simply look at me somberly, willing me to understand.

Ultimately, I did.

CHAPTER FORTY-SEVEN

JERUSALEM
Claudia Procula

I was living my dream. These faces of the people were so familiar they felt like family, the sounds made by their open mouths
unheard by the mounted Roman soldiers.

Gracian and the rest were leading our carriage through
the city of Jerusalem on the way to the palace. On the way to see
Lucius. Even the colors of the scarves were the same as in the
dreams I'd had for years. At first, they resembled eerily colored
butterflies, until our carriage drew close enough to see that they
were scarves. Half-standing in the small space, I craned my head
to look outside of the carriage, but I did so carefully, mindful of
my previous mishap. I had no intention of cracking my skull
again as a result of my insatiable curiosity.

These people were excited, joyous, and it certainly was not
because of us. I wondered why. What could cause so many people to pour into the streets, smiling and jostling one another excitedly? It was like *Saturnalia in April.*

I carefully negotiated the small wooden frame of the
window and sat back down on the carriage bench. "What do you

think they are celebrating, Antonia?" I asked my companion.

"The Jewish Passover is near. Esther told me that Jesus and his followers were making their way into Jerusalem. Perhaps he is already here!" Her eyes glowed as she smiled at me.

I was proud of my answering smile. *Do not think about the days ahead. Concentrate solely on Lucius. You will see him soon Claudia, after over eight months apart. Hold this precious, anticipatory joy close.*

CHAPTER FORTY-EIGHT

JERUSALEM
Lucius Pontius Pilate

Claudia would arrive soon. I felt both relieved and regretful at my acquiescence to Quintillus's repeated suggestions to bring her here. I was relieved because I needed her peaceful confidence; remorseful over the peril I could be placing her in. Although she was not yet twenty-one, my wife was wiser than almost anyone I knew—the sole exception being Quintillus, of course.

My mind reeled after the debacle of the day before, caused by the entry of the man they call Jesus into Jerusalem. Longinus, left in charge by Quintillus, had burst into my chambers where I lay exhausted by sleeplessness and an unrelenting sense of portent.

"SIR! Come please!" The usually perfectly groomed soldier had not shaved for at least two days and had not slept for at least that long. His hair was unkempt and dark eyes wide, the skin underneath bruised.

Jumping up, I threw on my toga praetexta almost laughing as I thought back to the days when I'd been proud of those purple vertical stripes. I'd believed they mattered—that I could actually accomplish something in Judea. Perhaps even bring peace.

Longinus flew down the steps of the palace ahead of me, through the courtyard, and out onto the main street. As I caught up with him, I encountered hundreds—perhaps thousands—of people lining the street, stretching eastward toward the old city. The din of their voices confused me.

Was this the riot that Caiaphas and Annas had feared for the past five years? These people are not just from Jerusalem. I hear Coptic, Syriac, Germanic, Aramaic, as well as Hebrew… and their voices sound joyous. This is no mob—these people are carrying on as if welcoming a hero or king!

As I watched, the crowd threw palm fronds and poplar branches onto the street in front of them, as if to form a carpet. As Longinus and I walked cautiously into the throng, no one even noticed us—we were invisible. Everyone's attention was on a figure approaching on a horse. No, not a horse—something smaller. As the figure and beast grew closer, I could see that this was Jesus, the man about whom Caiaphas and Annas had been increasingly frantic.

Before I could get a clear view of him, he turned his mount left toward the temple. Without thinking, I started to follow, until Longinus put his hand on my arm. He and I locked eyes for a moment as I marveled at the energy in the air; it fairly crackled as the throng breathed out audibly, as one. Their awe and joy were tangible as if they were connected in some mysterious way to the man who I now saw was riding a *donkey colt!*

Amidst the cacophony of languages, I could hear *alleluias* and the *hosannas*, as if this man was a god.

Hosanna!
Blessed is He who comes in the name of the Lord,
The King of Israel!

They were calling him *King, Lord*…but what kind of god

chooses a young donkey upon which to make his triumphal entry?

It was all so strange…and yet, I could not deny the yearning I felt, deep within. There was no other word for the feeling but *yearning*. It was a hunger for something I hadn't known I lacked.

CHAPTER FORTY-NONE

JERUSALEM
Lucius Pontius Pilate

"I have missed you, my bride. You have no idea how deeply." I felt at peace for the first time in many weeks. I tried to convince myself that it was simply the sexual release that had calmed me, but I knew my need for this woman was far more than a physical one. I wondered, not for the first time, if it was the same for her. I suspected it was not.

We lay in each other's arms in the vast expanse of the prelate chambers of the Jerusalem palace. Herod's vision and engineering skill had produced an even more wondrous edifice than my own palace in Caesarea—easily twice the size—yet I could never relax here. The massive building required more than one hundred servants and slaves to keep it in order, most of whom I had not bothered to learn the names of. There were quarters for over a thousand guests—one hundred in one of the towers alone. The high walls surrounding the place lent it more an impression of a fortress than a home. Herod must have feared an assault from the Hebrews.

I reveled in calling Claudia *my bride* after five years of

marriage, and she smiled as she always did at the term. She remained as much a mystery to me at that moment as she had been when we met. Her deep brown eyes were luminous as she held my gaze. As always, I felt bathed in her love. And yet...there was a way in which she was a total stranger to me. In all this time, I had learned nothing about how she thought or even what she thought about. When we were together, her attention was always on me and the challenges of our Judean landscape.

"Have you eaten, Lucius?"

I loved the sound of her voice because she spoke so rarely, and always toward a simple purpose. She never volunteered an opinion and expressed herself succinctly even when pushed for her views. My wife was clearly more comfortable with silence than with words, and I'd grown to love that quality, right along with all rest of the conundrum that was Claudia Procula.

Her Latin was flawless, almost musical in its cadence; I had long ago stopped listening for a Greek accent. I shook my head in response to her question, as I hadn't eaten since the previous evening.

Shaking her head in mock criticism, she arose from our bed, fully unadorned, and walked slowly and unselfconsciously over to the table where she had thrown her tunic. Languorously, she arranged the cloth over her body. Despite the pregnancies, her stomach was flat, breasts full and taut. Her long, dark hair hung past her waist, thick and glossy with light-brown, almost blonde highlights at her crown—from the sun, no doubt.

"I'm going to find us some supper, Lucius. I'll be back soon. Please rest until I return. You look extremely tired."

She wasn't wrong—even my bones ached with weariness. This assignment had been far more taxing than any of the wars or combatants I had ever faced. I felt increasingly more hopeless, the longer I stayed in Jerusalem.

"Look what Sabu has prepared for us, Lucius!"

Startled out of my morose ruminations, I looked up to see Sabu enter with several other servants and busily clear off a table to make room for what looked to be a heavenly repast.

Claudia watched me, her eyes dancing with delight. In spite of myself, I smiled. *Sabu, you are a trusted, familiar face. Claudia has brought you here knowing of my affection for you.*

CHAPTER FIFT

JERUSALEM
Claudia Procula

I knew Lucius felt remorseful about bringing me down to Jerusalem. It was only natural, as he still thought of me as his child bride—and why not? He was nearing forty years of age, while I was not yet twenty-one. He sensed the growing danger, the relentless clashing of the supernatural with the worldly powers in this place that reminded me of so very much of Delphi. Not geographically, of course, but in that both cities faced predestined battles. Delphi's was ending, and soon it would be a mere shrine, but Jerusalem's wars were on the horizon; they would become all-consuming and eternal.

My beloved husband needed me here. There was work I could do for him and his close allies. I felt, at my center, the impossible dyad of great sorrow and joy that marked the presence of truth.

Although I had not realized it at the time, Gracian, his soldiers, and the carriage carrying Antonia, Samu, and me had followed the exact path of the Righteous One, within thirty minutes of his own journey. The procession of He whom I had been

178

dreaming about since I was a child had been an occasion of un-trammeled joy. His welcome had been heralded by a profusion of colorful scarves thrown onto the very road we traveled.

Although I did not know each detail of what would take place, I knew that our lives as we knew them would end in just under a week.

The Oracle had prepared me. And I was ready.

CHAPTER FIFTY-ONE

JERUSALEM

Lucius Pontius Pilate

Quintillus burst into our chambers sometime around three in the morning. "They have arrested him, Lucius," he said unceremoniously, foregoing any apology for the untimely disturbance.

"Who?" I asked although I knew. The cloak of dread that had been tracking me for days now wrapped itself around me like a dear friend.

"Caiaphas has him at his palace and is planning to bring him here to you."

Claudia and I had jumped out of bed at the sound of the door of the anteroom of our chambers crashing open. I was searching frantically for my tunic. Already clothed in a peplos she kept hanging on the bedpost, Claudia handed my tunic to me with a serene smile. Leaving her hand on mine for a long moment, I sensed but could not see her eyes and the tranquility they conveyed.

How is it that I have been so blessed by the gods to have a woman like you?

I joined Quintillus on the veranda, where we could see

Caiaphas's palace lit with what looked like hundreds of torches and lamps.

"Jesus is from Galilee. That is the jurisdiction of Antipas. I will send him there."

My good friend nodded and remained silent as we stood looking out at the Jerusalem night, aware that we were caught up in a vortex of forces.

"Might any of that material sent by Seneca be of use to you now?"

I was surprised at the mention of a man Quintillus thought to be duplicitous at worst, hypocritical at best. But I was thankful for the reminder: in my confusion, I had forgotten that I possessed the story of this God of the Hebrews and his single-minded pursuit of them over all other peoples. Seneca had generously included the entire Mosaic Law with the writings he had sent about these fractious, long-oppressed Jews.

I smiled and took a deep breath. I extended my right hand to Quintillus, and when he grasped it, I pulled him toward me and whispered, "No matter how this ends for me, my friend, know that you have made this entire adventure possible." Feeling him stiffen and begin to pull away, I tightened my hold and hissed, "Listen to me. Without you at my side, I never could have done it. Any of it."

That I was speaking in past tense, neither of us acknowledged. We both understood in that instant that there could be only one end. Holding on to the best and only friend of my life, I asked the impossible of him. Impossible to think...and to say, "Quintillus, ...my trusted friend. Whe..." I stopped myself from saying it. "If... the worst happens, will you take care of Claudia?"

His answering embrace took my breath away.

CHAPTER FIFTY-TWO

JERUSALEM
Lucius Pontius Pilate

Just before dawn, two of Caiaphas's messengers appeared in the courtyard. I met them on the stairs, feeling no reason for any further political posturing.

"Why did Caiaphas send you here to me?"

"Because of the man Jesus."

The men were young and heavily bearded, according to their custom. Although neither looked older than Claudia, their eyes already bore the signs of the scholar. Fine lines radiated from the corners and between their eyes from hours of concentrated study through magnifying lenses to more easily read the scrolls. I knew the value of those lenses. Sabu's discovery of them for poring over tax receipts had been an unexpected boon for me during the hours I'd spent on the scrolls Seneca had sent.

We stood in silence, I two steps above them, as seconds stretched into minutes. I looked over their heads at the morning sun beginning to cast an ethereal glow over the upper city of Jerusalem and the golden cupolas of the temple. *Such a splendid sight. Far too sublime for man.*

I realized that I felt no anger toward these men—felt nothing at all, really. They were soldiers, not much different from me.

The taller of the two finally spoke, stammering badly from nerves. Neither the other messenger nor I understood a word he said.

After three futile attempts at disgorging his message, the man lifted up his hands in frustration, bowed his head, and descended several steps. His short, squat colleague then spoke softly, in a surprisingly deep voice. "The High Priest asks that you join in the interrogation against the man Jesus. Caiaphas invites you to his home…now."

"Rome has no conflict with this man," I replied. "We have heard his words and find nothing in what he says to indicate that he opposes Caesar. Tell Caiaphas that I will not fulfill his request."

The men stood looking up at me, their mouths half open, their faces illuminated by the rays of the rising sun.

"S-S-Sir, p-p-please. C-C-C-Come with us. P-P-P-Please," managed the taller man. I recognized the signs of desperation. They'd clearly been threatened with severe punishment if they were to fail to deliver me.

"Give me paper and quill, and I will tell the priests myself," I said, guessing that they might carry such things. Sure enough, the stammerer instantly pulled out both, then practically raced up the stairs separating us to hand them to me.

I asked him to present his back, and wrote out a message while bracing the scroll against it:

Caiaphas and Annas,

My trusted centurion has heard this man Jesus speak. His words contain no threat to the Princeps Tiberius or to the Roman Empire. In fact, he advises respect for the Empire. We have no quarrel with this man.

*Should you decide to force this issue, it is
my understanding that the man called Jesus is
a citizen of Galilee, and therefore subject to the
jurisdiction of Herod Antipas. I know that Antipas is in Jerusalem for your Passover celebration so it would seem that asking him to deal
with the man—rather than I—would be the best
and easiest course.*

*I will not participate in any jurisdictional
conflict against the Nazarene.*

The message would merely buy me time, I knew this.
However, if Fortuna smiled on me, I'd have enough time to review the pertinent facts of Hebrew history, and perhaps discover
the most effective way to pressure Annas and Caiaphas to back
down.

I was so engrossed in my thoughts as I climbed the stairs
that I nearly collided with Claudia on the veranda.

CHAPTER FIFTY-THREE

Lucius Pontius Pilate

"Lucius, they are coming. I count fourteen, including the high priest, walking through the courtyard."

Claudia stood at the doorway of the room I had fashioned into an office. I lay stretched out on the *lectus lucubratorius*, surrounded by numerous scrolls.

"You remind me of myself many years ago, husband, when I'd recline on a similar couch surrounded by Uncle Adrian's collection of Plato's *Dialogues*."

Her smile was forced. She held a cup and a small plate in her hands. Holding them out, she said, "Please, Lucius, eat. Drink. Sabu prepared some bread and cheese, and just a small amount of diluted wine. Not enough to dull your senses."

Her first words made me jump. I had been deeply focused on the exotic story of a people chosen by God and led out of Egypt amidst such miracles as the parting of the sea and the smiting of first-born sons. When I swung my legs to the floor to stand, several scrolls dropped from my lap.

Claudia placed the food and beverage on a table and

quickly retrieved the papers. Gently, she placed her hands on my forearms and leaned in to kiss my cheek, her dark eyes glistening with unshed tears. Even after the miscarriages, I had never seen Claudia cry. Looking into those eyes, I could see my own pain reflected there.

"Please, Lucius. You have had nothing to eat since yesterday afternoon."

I nodded and tried to swallow the knot of emotion in my throat so that I might obey her wishes. She was so young and yet ageless. I never grew tired of enumerating my bride's qualities, one of the rarest of which was that she lived wholly in the present. I knew the loss of our babies had hurt her deeply. Her excitement at the pregnancies had been genuine and fervent, and yet— afterward—she never spoke of it. She would have made a superb mother.

The serenity of Claudia's countenance, the beauty of her form, were unlike any I had ever seen, let alone bedded. Gazing into the light that seemed to emanate from her eyes, I could read the understanding there, the vast tide of wise words she held in her heart. Sometimes I could almost hear them as we kissed.

We sat together, knee touching knee, as I drank the wine and managed to consume more than half of the bread and cheese. Then, simultaneously, we stood and placed ourselves almost toe to toe. One large tear dropped from Claudia's eye and slowly traced a path toward the right side of her parted lips. I kissed it away and, without a word, walked out the door to meet those who awaited me. I could not look back. There was no solace I could offer my wife.

CHAPTER FIFTY-FOUR

Lucius Pontius Pilate

It took me almost five minutes, moving apace, to traverse the vast distance from my chambers to the area between the east and west wings reserved for adjudication. As I walked, I grew calmer. Perhaps it was the light drink that had eased my nerves. Ever wise in her ministrations, Claudia must have known something momentous was coming, just as I did. It was inevitable and, perversely, it was a relief. There would be no more wondering *if* or *when.* I suspected she felt the same.

There were indeed fourteen men outside the palace, edgily awaiting my arrival at the *preatorium*, the place of Roman judgment. As I walked out to meet them, I closed the two massive doors tightly, surprised at the effort it took. Their tremendous weight perfectly mirrored my feelings.

Jewish beliefs prohibited the men from entering the palace, which would render them "ritually unclean"—and therefore unfit to partake in the Passover feast.

I sat in the *solium*—a most uncomfortable seat, I thought wryly. It was intended, I was sure, to encourage governors to make swift work of disputes over trivial matters. The armrests were golden eagle wings that extended from a solid-gold band supporting the chair's wooden bottom. The intended effect was one of intimidation of the supplicant. Before me stood Annas and Caiaphas, Summas, Datam, Gamaliel, Judas, Levi, Nepthalim, Alexander, Cyrus…and four others whose names I forgot the moment they were uttered.

"We are assured that this man Jesus—who calls himself the son of God—is born of fornication," said one of the four unknowns. "He is said to be the son of Joseph the carpenter, and a woman named Mary." The elder's beard and hair were white and he wore a small box on his wrist.

So these men must be members of the Sanhedrin, the court of seventy-one rulers, scribes, priests and rabbis who rule this place.

Speaking in Greek, the old man pressed on. "He advocates the dissolution of the Sabbath and other laws of our fathers. Not only that, but he calls himself a *king*. Clearly, he presents an imminent threat to Rome and to Tiberius Caesar."

And so it begins.

My mind was clear, and I felt confident in my ability to prevail in this verbal skirmish—for a time, anyway.

"What does he declare, exactly?" I asked. "And what is it that he attempts to dissolve?"

A younger man chimed in. "He claims to cure the deaf, blind, and lame, the demoniacs—those afflicted with palsy and leprosy—all without regard to our prohibition of performing cures on the Sabbath. These actions he performs through wickedness, of that I am sure."

There was an interesting hierarchy in play. The four whose names I had forgotten were assigned to offer these preliminary accusations. Perhaps Caiaphas and Annas intended to speak last—or not at all.

I realized as I posed my next question that I was honestly

curious about the answer. "How can these things be done through wickedness?"

"He is a conjurer," replied a third of the tribunal. "His ability to cast out devils comes from the power of the prince of devils himself."

The looks of consternation on the faces of the four who had been thrown to the Roman wolf were pathetic. I felt sorry for them...almost.

Casting out devils with the power of the prince of devils...how can that make sense? Would a devil cast himself out? They were reaching. Making it up as they went along.

"Casting out devils would not seem to proceed from an unclean spirit, but would be the work of God, would it not?" I felt a surge of energy as I recalled what I had read in Seneca's second scroll. "Moreover, did your Moses not predict that there would rise up a prophet from among your brethren? That he would look like you, and that your God would put words in his mouth? That he would speak all that was commanded of him by God?"

This was too easy, these boys were laying their own traps.

I must have been doing too well. Caiaphas stepped forward. "Procurator," he said, bowing deeply, his tone unctuous.

Here it comes. These High Priests are far more skilled at endless debate than I. They have spent their lives at it, after all. I should be grateful to have held them for even a few moments.

"We entreat you, Procurator, to summon this Jesus so that you can question him yourself. If this man were not an evildoer, we would not have handed him over."

I had been expecting this...so why the sudden jolt at the thought of meeting this man? Do I fear my own death? No, it's not that, I've long thought I would not live to see my fortieth birthday. It's...something else.

I forced myself to quiet my thoughts and respond. "You did send him to Herod Antipas, per my instructions, did you not?"

"We did."

"Then, please tell me, why are you here?"

In the silence that followed my question, I glanced away from Caiaphas and was dismayed to see the courtyard below filling with people. More than a hundred, maybe two hundred were already there, watching and hoping to hear snippets of our conversation. Their presence was not accidental. The Sanhedrin had been busy that morning, stirring up trouble among people who, a mere week before, had been jubilant at the entry into the city of the Nazarene. The sun had risen. I surmised the time to be around eight in the morning. I shifted my weight and stared back at Caiaphas.

"Herod questioned him, your Excellency," he responded finally. "As did we. But he would answer none of our questions. Herod asks that you judge him for yourself."

I could imagine the foolish and frivolous line of inquiry that must have spouted from Antipas. The man was incapable of understanding anything but his own insatiable appetites. The truth was, I had hoped to forestall this meeting far longer. The extreme dread I felt at facing Jesus threatened to overwhelm me—but there was nothing more I could say. Caiaphas had artfully laid the fate of this man at my feet.

Just as I opened my mouth to speak, I saw a curtain in the lower level of the Tower of David flutter, and then, the face of my Claudia. As far away as she was, somehow I could see the perfect serenity of her expression.

The darkness began to fade. The words of Cicero on the obligations of civil service returned to me:

Men who in a civil capacity direct the affairs of the nation render no less important service that those who conduct its wars. . . . Diplomacy in the friendly settlement of controversies is more desirable than courage in settling them on the battlefield. . . . It takes a brave and resolute spirit not to be disconcerted in times of difficulty or ruffled and thrown off one's feet, as they say, but to keep one's presence of mind and one's self-possession and not to swerve from the path of reason. Now all this requires great personal courage; but it also calls for great intellectual ability by reflection to anticipate the future, to discover some time in advance what is going to happen, whether for good or ill, and what must be done in any possible event, and never to be reduced to having to say, "I hadn't thought of that." . . . There are, therefore, instances of civic courage that are not inferior to the courage of the soldier. Indeed, [civic service] calls for even greater energy and even greater devotion.

This was just a different type of death from that which I had faced so many times on the battlefield.

"Bring him here," I said.

CHAPTER FIFTY-FIVE

Claudia Procula

As I watched from my perch in the tower, my heart broke for Lucius...for all that he had endured and all that he would continue to undergo. And yet, I was filled with pride for my husband as well: for the steadfast, earnest lucidity with which he conducted his interrogation of these messengers of the High Priest, and for his willingness to change his view of these people.

Like most Romans, Lucius had found the beliefs of the Jews alien, even incongruous. The more time he'd spent with Caiaphas, the more farcical he'd found the disjunction between what the priest professed and what he practiced. For years, he had spoken of his frustration with these self-proclaimed holy people and their patent hypocrisies.

But, over these past few days, since my arrival in Jerusalem, I learned that Lucius's attitude had changed. Long into the nights, he had talked about his contrition over the deaths of the boys in Caesarea. He had shed tears as he told me of his visit to their mothers, and his vain hope that he might be attacked by the Jews in retaliation—maybe even killed. Mainly, though, his tears flowed at the thought of the rabbi who had forced the mourners to hold themselves in check. Lucius had seen the nobility of this man who could, even when embedded in justifiable outrage, counsel forgiveness.

It felt like a gift when he'd explained that all of his anger, frustration, and resentment against the Judean people had melted away, replaced by a new level of understanding and compassion. "Claudia," he'd explained, "it was during my months of digging through the hard-packed desert ground, engaged in grueling labor the likes of which I had never experienced, that I was freed."

I will remember until I die the look on my husband's face when I walked into his study to find him almost obscured by piles of Mosaic scrolls. He had been at it all night...had never come to bed, and he honestly looked like a boy of twelve. The best way I can explain it is that his face was suffused with the light of understanding.

"Claudia, I see!" he'd said triumphantly. "Caiaphas, Annas, and their predecessors were given a virtually impossible task: to preserve not just the religious beliefs but the traditions, culture, and veritable *life* of an entire race. And they were tasked with doing this in the face of successive oppression by rulers from far and wide. We Romans are merely the latest in a very long list of those who have subjugated the Jews. No wonder they behave as they do. They are striving to maintain the strange, divisive, chaotic, yet perversely stable balance of power among their own factions."

He bowed his head and sat quietly for a moment, and when he spoke again, his exhilaration had given way to exhaustion. "It is the way of all men, isn't it, my bride?"

Few men would have had the capacity for a change of heart this profound—but Lucius was not like other men. I thought back to our first year of marriage when his sometimes ruthless treatment of the Hebrews had frightened me on occasion. I also recalled the high esteem in which he had held the Roman Senator Seneca—a man about whom I did not try to conceal my disdain. From the moment I'd first seen him on the ship from Athens, I'd feared and loathed him.

Seneca's writings, which Lucius had thought so highly of, were, in fact, a conglomerate of the ideas of Zeno of Citium, Simonides, and Epictetus—all of whom I had studied with Uncle Adrian. That Seneca had taken the thoughts of these great men and rewritten them as his own showed a dangerous, careless arrogance. When Lucius had decided to parade the military standard with the Caesar Tiberius's image and Roman golden eagle throughout Caesarea, I'd suspected the idea had emanated from the discourses of Seneca on how to control the Jews. It had been the first of many times in our marriage when I had been tempted to override the wisdom of the Oracle and endeavor to change Lucius's mind. If he had not done such a flagrantly disrespectful thing, surely, there would have been no riot on that day. But, even if Lucius been unrelentingly respectful of the Hebrews, agreeable and pliable for all these five years, this day would surely have dawned. This I knew.

I do not think I ever loved him more than I did on that day...a day that would stretch into eternity.

The day that marked the beginning of the end.

CHAPTER FIFTY-SIX

Lucius Pontius Pilate

I stood as the four priests brought Jesus before me.

He looked like an ordinary man—until I dared look into his eyes. Then I wondered why I was standing. He was taller than most; almost my height. They had clad him in an ostentatiously elaborate white robe, feminine in its design. *The garment was the work of Antipas,* I thought as he climbed up the stairs toward me, *meant to humiliate him.* The effect was quite the opposite.

When our eyes locked, I felt that jolt again, this time right down to my core. I felt *known* in a way I had never been before—not even by Claudia. The growing crowd, the priests, everything receded from my sight, and I was aware only of this man, of the endlessness of his gaze, of its penetration into my soul.

At the sound of stones dropping onto the cement courtyard, I looked up. Caiaphas had dropped a handful of rocks. *He did that deliberately. He knows the power of this man and fears it. This is a man who speaks the word of God. His God. This is a man who prays at his own temple.*

"What do you accuse this man of?" I said to Caiaphas.

"If he were not a criminal, we would not be handing him over to you," he replied, drawing himself up to his full height. He had no interest in repeating his accusations in front of the man and was cross with me for compelling him to do so—to do the dirty work he'd sooner leave to one of his minions. I could see the muscles in his jaw tense. Maybe if his anger took him over, he would lose his focus.

"We caught this man misleading our people, telling them not to pay taxes to Caesar. Even more egregious, he claims to be *Christ*—a king."

"Well then, you yourselves should take him and try him according to your own law," I said, in one last attempt to exempt myself from this fatal action. *Let's pretend that we have never covered this territory, Caiaphas. I can overlook the fact that you are lying about his telling the people not to pay their taxes. He has never said anything of the kind. In fact, has supported payment to Caesar. I know you will eventually win this verbal jousting match, but, by Jove, I will resist you and your ends as far as the god's permit.*

"It is against our laws to put anyone to death, Procurator."

Oh, Caiaphas, have you no shame? Is there no end to your deceit and manipulation? Is nothing too base for you? This man who would heal a dying slave on the Sabbath? You would like to see this innocent man put to death—and yet you call me and my fellow Romans pagans?

I turned and beckoned my soldiers to bring Jesus inside the palace.

CHAPTER FIFTY-SEVEN

Lucius Pontius Pilate

We stood face to face. Jesus gazed at me as if we were standing in a garden or on a beach, with a total absence of fear, anger, or even resentment. His countenance was wholly serene.

It is as if...as if he really were a king. Or a god.

We were about the same age, or perhaps he was a year or two younger than I. Even in the ludicrous robe, nobility seemed to emanate from his every pore.

Who are you?

"Are you the king of the Jews?" I asked, attempting to keep my voice even.

"Do you ask this on your own, or have others told you?"

Ask this on my own? Instantly, I thought of Quintillus's story about meeting Jesus several days earlier. He'd taken an incalculable risk by stopping and telling the prophet about his servant, who was dying with fever. The servant had recovered completely by the time Quintillus returned to the barracks.

He knows what I am thinking. He can hear my thoughts as if I were speaking them. And yet, there is no trace of arro-

gance, belligerence, or condescension about him. I had never before experienced such overwhelming kindness and forgiveness. I felt bathed in his mercy.

He was slight of build but wiry. He looked like a working man. When he shifted his stance, the sleeves of his robe slipped back to reveal muscular forearms. Olive-skinned, he looked like a man who had spent hours in the desert sun.

But those eyes. His eyes looked almost black one moment, then seemed to change to a greenish-blue as I stared. They were every color I had ever seen, warm and inviting. Those were laugh lines at the corners of his mouth; he had clearly smiled and laughed his share during his thirty-something years.

Say something, Lucius!

"I am not a Jew, am I? I know nothing about your people or your customs! It is your own nation and its chief priests who have handed you over to me. What have you done?"

Eyes still locked on mine, he replied, "My kingdom does not belong to this world. If my kingdom did belong to this world, my attendants would be fighting to keep me free. But, as it is, my kingdom is not here."

His Greek was flawless. Where had a working man learned to speak the language of the most educated Romans and Greeks?

My kingdom is not here...

I understood full well that this man was not speaking of a worldly realm. Not knowing how to respond, I said, "Then, you believe you are a king?"

There was a movement behind the curtain, and I knew Claudia was there, listening. The thought brought me deep consolation. It was clear that I had lost my strange verbal joust with Caiaphas, but neither of us would emerge a winner in the larger battle. This man would be victorious—that was preordained. Caiaphas and I were merely playing our parts. Somehow, my child bride knew all this, too. She and I had very little time left together. This, she had understood since I'd met her.

"You say I am a king," said the man in response to my question. "For this I was born and for this I came into the world, to testify to the truth. Everyone who belongs to the truth listens to my voice."

Truth. That which we all seek from the moment we arrive at the age of reason, and never fully attain.

I held back what I wanted to say—what I wanted to ask—and instead asked simply, "What *is* truth?"

There was a flicker of what looked like disappointment in those omnicolored eyes before his mouth moved into a half smile and his face filled with compassion and pity. "Truth is from heaven," he said so low I could barely hear him.

"Then truth is not on earth?"

"Believe that truth is on earth among those who have the power of right judgment, are governed by truth, and form right judgment."

His words burned. Who would speak like this? Who could know these words?

I turned away from him abruptly and threw open the double doors to the courtyard. I stalked out and shouted to the crowd, which had quadrupled in size, "I find no fault in this man!"

I scanned the crowd of thousands. *Where had they all come from?* I spotted Caiaphas and Annas near the back of the courtyard. They had found a sculpture with a base wide enough to stand on so they might have a view of me over the top of the assembled multitude. They looked smug, confident.

While staring at the two High Priests, I played my last card. Raising my voice to the crowd, I said, "I understand that you all have a custom on Passover. Each year, the Procurator releases one prisoner. Do you want me to release to you the King of the Jews?"

As if in one mad voice, the crowd cried, "No! Not this

one! Release Barabbas!"

If I released Jesus, there would be a riot that would make all others pale in comparison.

So be it. I would have him scourged. Surely that would be adequate bloodshed for these people.

But I knew I was deceiving myself. Again.

CHAPTER FIFTY-EIGHT

Claudia Procula

It went on for a lifetime. Several lifetimes. The man could barely kneel, never mind stand, as two massive men took turns flailing him with short, three-thonged leather whips embedded with chunks of iron, zinc, and bone. Both arms chained about a column, his body lay against its base, legs motionless on the ground. He did not utter a cry.

I knew Lucius had not approved the doubling of the usual twenty lashes, nor could he possibly have known the extent of the carnage. His wounds were beyond description and the volume of blood loss seemed incompatible with life. I thought I could see bone where muscle had once been. These were not Roman soldiers, these torturers. They were too corpulent. Perhaps they were Idumeans...or Carthaginians.

I do not know what compelled me to watch a scene I had been envisioning since my days with the Oracle. I was prepared for the outcome, of course: I knew this man/god would be killed. The foreknowledge did nothing to make the scene less horrifying.

201

Finally, they took him away. How he stayed on his feet is a mystery. And then I saw her—the woman who had been standing at the periphery of the jeering, mocking crowd. She'd remained silent throughout the bloody scene, watching, waiting. Once the "entertainment" was over and the crowd began to disperse, she crept forward, removed her robe, and ripped it into three long strips. With these cloths, she began to clean...no... that's not what she was doing. She was *collecting his blood.*

I plucked up some towels, as many as I could find, and raced down the three flights and out into the east side of the courtyard, which was now nearly empty but for her.

Without a word, I knelt down next to her and handed her half of the towels. From beneath the hood of her light-blue tunic, her steady gaze met mine without curiosity or surprise. My dress was similar to hers, right down to the hood covering my hair; she could not have known who I was as I knelt beside her in the blood of her son.

It was obvious that she was his mother. They had the same shape face, the same dark hair and almond eyes. I knew she must have been several decades older than I, but her skin was smooth, unflawed by age or sun. There were lines at the far corners of her eyes, the residue of happier times, and her expression? I recognized it as wisdom. For a split second, her face transformed into that of the Oracle at Delphi...but when I blinked, I was looking once again into the face of the mother of Jesus.

Kneeling next to her, helping her soak up the blood of her son, I thought about the first of the three perfect baby boys I had miscarried; the child Lucius would never know existed. It came to pass while he was at one of those endless meetings with Caiaphas and Annas, accompanied by oceans of blood—just as now. But that blood was mostly my own.

Now, two mothers, eyes wet with tears, knelt in a son's blood, watching as it painted the bottoms of our tunics crimson.

CHAPTER FIFTY-NINE

JERUSALEM
Lucius Pontius Pilate

That he could make his way up the stairs to me was impossible—and yet, he did it, step after excruciating step. There was a crown of vicious thorns digging into his scalp and a purple cloak thrown over the dreadful wounds made visible by an occasional breeze that lifted the ends of the garment.

Quintillus had returned and stood to my right, his face a study in pain as he watched the man called Jesus struggle up the stairs.

I flung open the doors of the portico and led him out. "*Ecce homo!*" I shouted. *Behold the man.* My men—poor excuses for soldiers all—had tortured him sadistically, beyond all reason. He could barely see past the streams of blood that flowed from the deep wounds made by his crown of thorns.

"Look! I have brought him out to you, so you know I find no guilt in this man."

"Hail, King of the Jews!" the crowd shouted back.

But from the eastern side of the courtyard came a horrifying cry: "CRUCIFY HIM! CRUCIFY HIM! FREE BARABBAS!"

It was Caiaphas, Annas, and their fellow priests and temple guards.

"Take him yourselves and crucify him!" I shouted at them. "I find no guilt in him!"

How I wished to be back in Germania, engaged in battle. If only Quintillus had not saved my life that day, had let the soldier poised over me thrust his sword into my heart. Another three seconds and I would not have survived to find myself in this terrible place, vainly defending a man who had done nothing but heal the sick and preach forgiveness and love. It seemed there was no place for unalloyed goodness in this world—certainly not among priests.

Caiaphas spoke. "We have a law, and according to that law, no man may make himself out to be the son of God. This Jesus has done so, and must die for it."

He could stop this. Why doesn't he strike us all down?

My dilemma was an excruciating one. I had two wholly opposing obligations. Standing in front of me was a man whom I *knew* to be innocent of any wrongdoing, who in fact seemed capable only of doing good. The killing of innocents was not new to me; it was too often an unfortunate consequence of war. But this man was no ordinary man, and he had made extraordinary enemies. Caiaphas and his cohort considered him so great a threat that they would do anything to assure his disgrace and death.

My oath as a legionary had been to carry out all commands of the Emperor without question. That vow had not been annulled with my promotion to Procurator of Judea; on the contrary, it had taken on heft. My primary responsibility now was assuring that Judean taxes flowed to Rome. The financial demands on the Empire were massive and grew with each new conquest. If I did not satisfy the blood lust of these crafty Hebrew priests, they would foment a kind of chaos that would interfere with the order of things—and that most certainly included the obligation of paying taxes.

How I yearn for the bloody but clearly demarcated fields of battle, where things were simple: I led my soldiers into combat knowing full well the day might be my last. The worst outcome possible was death, and that was never something I feared. There are far worse things than an honorable death. Worst of all would be to shirk my obligation to the Emperor...to the Empire.

I turned back to look upon the battered and bloody countenance before me. "Where are you from?" I asked as I led him back inside the palace again. *Who are you?*

Mutely, he stared back at me and I sensed sorrow and pity emanating from him. For me. *Here you stand, beaten, bleeding, ridiculed, and yet you pity me?*

"Do you not speak to me?" I pressed.

He remained silent.

"Do you not understand that I have the power to release you?" The lie burned my mouth, the words were caustic on my lips. I saw Claudia's face through the curtain and was ashamed of my cravenness. *Lucius, you are nothing but a low-level tool of Caesar, no better than Sejanus and as much of a hypocrite as Seneca. You know you cannot release this man. These priests have the power, not you. If you try to let him go, there will be total anarchy...they will see to it.*

"You would have no power over me if it had not been given to you from above," he said quietly. "The greater sin belongs to those who handed me over to you."

His simple words matched his gentle countenance, but clashed mightily with the ruined state of his face and body.

He is speaking words of forgiveness! How is that possible?

In desperation, I cried out, "What shall I do with you!?"

I did not expect a reply, but through his cracked, bloody lips there came one. "You must act as it is written."

"How is it written?"

"Moses and the prophets have foretold my suffering and resurrection." His gaze was steady and he seemed unafraid, despite the trials he had already withstood and the weight of those to come.

Who are you? I wondered again. *No man calmly permits himself to be scourged, spit on, crucified!*

No MAN.

Two more times I went out and tried to reason with the crowd. The second time, I asked that Barabbas be brought to me in the hope that these people could see for themselves the error in their judgment. On my right stood Jesus and on my left, Barabbas, a known thief and murderer. The man acted deranged. His lips curled back and he spewed vile curses at the top of his lungs.

I reminded the crowd that their own prophets had predicted the coming of one such as the man who stood at my right. I pointed out that the man to my left was a common criminal, while Jesus had been hailed as the Holy One, the son of God, a mere six days earlier. "Shall I crucify your King?" I demanded.

The mob was a blur to me, but I could discern some faces that seemed to reflect distress. A few women were doubled over, sobbing with grief. But, just as I dared hope that I might turn the tide, the voices of Caiaphas and Annas rose above the rest, shouting, "We have no king but Caesar!"

Not even those most sympathetic to Jesus dared resist the power of the High Priests and the Sanhedrin. How could they?

It was over.

CHAPTER SIXTY

Claudia Procula

Five years passed so very quickly. Unbearably so.

It felt like just a few days earlier that I had gone to Delphi, nearly died from a concussion, then sailed from Athens to Caesarea to become the wife of Lucius Pontius Pilate.

I listened to the entire exchange between my husband and the man-God, Jesus. Each successive word they uttered plunged more deeply into my soul.

I felt hollowed out, emptier than I had after each miscarriage. I experienced pure, deep, desolation on that day, in spite of my preparation by the Oracle. Yes, I knew all that would happen...but imagining it had been nothing compared to the reality.

I felt white-hot hatred, not at the wily priests and certainly not at Lucius or Jesus. All of my wrath was directed at the God I knew existed. That One God was connected in some baffling way to this god-man in human form. Of course, the idea that a god might change form at will was not at all strange to me, having grown up in the world of Zeus, Apollo, Artemis, and countless other gods and goddesses. But this man—or whatever he was—referred to himself as both the son of god and the son of man. He was something completely outside my worldly experience...

Watching Lucius use his training, character, reason, and basic *goodness* to forestall the inevitable felt like watching the servants lay traps at Adrian's farm. Small animals, seeking a carrot or some green, would approach the snares...closer, closer, until...WHACK.

The blades dropped down to decapitate the innocent creatures.

Lucius's understanding of Mosaic law and his ability to articulate it with profound sincerity did move many in the courtyard. But just as it seemed he was beginning to change the hearts and minds of the crowd—just as they began to listen and think for themselves—Caiaphas or one of the temple guards would shout for blood. It did not even matter that what they shouted was irrelevant to what Lucius had just said. The effect was the same. The leaders were as intransigent as they were powerful. The people had no choice.

Lucius was not dead yet, but he would be. And soon.

What could Lucius have done differently? Could he—or anyone on earth—have stopped the horror that took place that day?

CHAPTER SIXTY-ONE

JERUSALEM
Lucius Pontius Pilate

It felt as if the entire city of Jerusalem would be destroyed. In the middle of that afternoon, it turned so dark, I couldn't see my hand before my face. Then the earth began to tremble, shaking the stones of the temple gently, then ferociously.

I will destroy this temple and, in three days, will raise it up again.

I hoped the entire structure would crumble. As I watched, the supporting platform atop the sixteen-foot retaining walls shook dangerously. The temple was the highest building in the city—intentionally so, as it was meant to be the home of the Hebrew God. King Herod had restored it with the help of architects from Greece, Rome, and Egypt after one of the many battles that razed it, along with the rest of the city.

Not that destroying the temple was easy; it was triple-walled to protect its inner sanctum from pagans like me. I could see the golden cornices of what they called the Holy of Holies rock from side to side. Would this grandiose tribute to their god withstand the earth's quaking?

Gracian had heard Jesus say it: *I will destroy this temple and in three days, will raise it up again.* He had also heard the priests mock the man: *Destroy Solomon's temple? And then raise it up again? This is the raving of a madman and a blasphemer.*

Evidently, the temple guards and priests had enjoyed many hours of amusement over this and the rest of the man's claims.

When dawn's light returned, I could see that a mere corner of an outside wall gate had been dislodged. The rest of Herod's temple stood intact and stable once more.

What had he meant by his strange proclamation?

I knew I should get back to Rome. After my unsuccessful attempt to win mercy for Jesus, I could not stay in the land of the Jews. By my actions, I had forfeited all claims of legal or judicial power. A Roman Prelate did not implore his subjects and continue to rule. I respected Tiberius—admired and felt obligated to him. I owed it to him to step aside. But there was something as yet unfinished in Jerusalem, and I could not leave just yet.

It took three days.

"Lucius, I asked them to tell you this themselves," Quintillus said. He was standing inside the palace accompanied by three impeccably uniformed Roman soldiers. These were the guards that had been placed before the cave where Jesus' body rested.

None of the men would meet my gaze. At first, I thought it merely a gesture of respect, but when I looked at them more closely, I could see they were troubled in some way; their posture was off...they emanated the subtle fragrance of failure. They looked just as I felt.

"What happened?" I demanded, a variety of potential horrors galloping through my mind.

Longinus—a courageous man I had known and trusted for years—supplied an answer, and it was far from anything I'd anticipated.

"The body is gone, sir."

Stupidly, I stared at him, then glanced at Quintillus, who was suppressing a smile. "You rolled a massive boulder in front of the grave, as I requested?"

"We did, sir."

"And there were guards there at all times? Awake? Watching?"

I sensed but did not see Quintillus's attitude change. He became tense as if preparing to defend the men.

"We were on the ground when we awakened, sir."

"On the ground when you awakened!" I understood now why Quintillus was so rigid. "Start from the beginning, please."

Longinus shifted from one foot to the other, coughed… cleared his throat, coughed again. "Sir…we saw a blinding light and then…" He paused, looking wholly miserable at the thought of telling a tale no one in his right mind would believe.

All I could think was, *I will destroy this temple, and in three days I will raise it up again.*

"Proceed, Longinus—what happened at that cave?"

"There were…the only way I can think to describe them is…'light-filled beings,' sir. They were at least twelve, maybe fifteen feet tall. Together, they lifted something that looked like a sword…." He paused and glanced down at his own sword hanging from his waist. "They aimed it at us and we fell unconscious. Or…at least that is the last thing I remember." He glanced back at his associates and they nodded. He then began speaking more quickly, as if he wanted to get the whole story out before he lost his nerve. "When we woke up, the boulder had been rolled away and the tomb was empty! We examined it thoroughly, but all it contained was the tunic that Jesus had worn when on the cross. Nothing more. No sign of the body, sir."

I couldn't find words so I simply stared at the man, who was breathing heavily. It was as if simply telling the story had been exhausting. After a moment, he continued. "The High Priests are accusing us of stealing the body and hiding it. And word of the…event…seems to have gripped the imaginations of the people. Some are claiming to have seen their dead relatives walking among them. The Priests insist that you triple our patrols through the city."

I blinked a few times as I tried to think of the proper response. Without any intention of doing so, I blurted out, "I will destroy this temple, and in three days I will raise it up again."

"Sir, I am sorry," said Longinus, "but…I don't understand."

Of course you don't!

He understood enough to feel relieved—this I could see written on his face. He may not have comprehended my words or where they came from, but he knew that I believed his preposterous story.

CHAPTER SIXTY-TWO

Lucius Pontius Pilate

More of his words drifted through my mind: *Believe that truth is on earth among those who have the power of right judgment, are governed by truth, and form right judgment.* His final words were a command: *Do as it is written.*

He had been insisting that I give up my fight for his life. *Because this is the death I choose...*

For the first time in over a week, I slept. I arose after twelve hours and asked Quintillus for his help. I had decided to do a final report for the Emperor. I knew Tiberius to be a man who respected the truth even when it came wrapped in controversy and enigma. All he demanded was the proper application of reason and logic.

Perhaps I was wrong about my own fate. It was possible that the Emperor would be receptive to my version of the catastrophic events in Jerusalem. Grasping at the possibility, I outlined my plan to Quintillus, along with my concern that Sejanus might intercept it. Then I asked my friend for his opinion.

His level gaze measured me. He took a long drought of

the diluted wine Sabu had poured for us and nodded his assent. "I think you are correct in assuming that the Emperor is unlikely to see your missive, Lucius. Sejanus will see to that; he's gained extraordinary power of late. Tiberius has once again fled Rome. He lives in Cyprus now, and will speak only with Sejanus."

I took a deep breath, held it, and thought of the piles of messages from Rome that lay unopened during the months I had been in Bethlehem.

My trusted confidant's eyes narrowed and grew dark. His mouth tightened. "And...there is more, my friend."

Tell me, Quintillus...just how bad is it?

"We intercepted a message from one of the temple guards. It was meant to go to Rome."

I smiled, knowing full well what *intercepted* meant. But my smile faded at Quintillus's next revelation. "Caiaphas claims that you stole from the Jerusalem Temple funds to finance the aqueduct."

Had I been standing, I would have staggered. The enormity of the lie stupefied me. Extortion of funds was a capital crime! Treason. For this alone, I could be executed. *Was there money missing? Had the monies sent by the Empire been stolen? Was it done by one of Sejanus's supporters...or was Caiaphas merely making this claim to ensure my demise?* I could not help thinking of Flaccus, our similarities eerily congruent, but I lacked a Cicero.

After a few moments of this kind of thinking, I realized there was no way to know the truth of what had happened, nor did it really matter. The fact that the message had been intercepted provided but a temporary reprieve; it was only a matter of time before another was written and reached Rome.

The power shift from Tiberius to Sejanus was potentially calamitous for me. That, along with Caiaphas's betrayal, meant the end of my career and probably my life. And yet I felt a strange sense of calm. My mission to investigate the execution of Jesus—undertaken out of my unshakeable loyalty to Tiberius Caesar—could be carried out more slowly and carefully now that the Emperor had all but ceded his authority to Sejanus. Instead of completing this clandestine inquiry in a week, I could remain in Jerusalem as long as a month or six weeks before returning to Rome. The end would be the same for me: I would take my own life because I had brought dishonor to the Empire. I had failed in my mission to keep the peace in Judea. The only control I had at this point was over where and how I chose to end my life. Before that end came, I would take the time to conduct a thorough investigation here.

I broke into my first genuine smile since my early days with Claudia. "Will you assist me in this last adventure, my friend?" I asked Quintillus.

His answering nod, steady gaze and evident eagerness were food for my soul.

Quintillus and I met with five of our most trusted men: the three who had been on watch over the tomb of Jesus, plus Gracian and Marcus, who had been with us for years. These five we entrusted with our true purpose and the reason we'd doubled the patrols around the city: to seek out the testimony of anyone willing to share stories of Jesus—the Christ, as he had come to be called. No patrol went out without one of the five as a leader.

CHAPTER SIXTY-THREE

Quintillus and I went to speak with Joseph of Arimathea, the wealthy Hebrew who had come to ask me for the body two nights previously. He had offered his tomb as a burial site for Jesus, and I felt he'd be a prudent place to begin my investigation.

Joseph's home was in the upper city, a long but welcome walk from the palace. In an attempt at anonymity, both Quintillus and I wore the headdress and robes of the Jews as we hurried through the busy streets.

Joseph and another man stood on the porch of his large marble home. Noting our cautious approach, Joseph walked rapidly down to us and explained in low tones, "This is my friend Nicodemus." After a quick glance in both directions, he added, "Come in quickly."

We were soon enjoying tea and bits of honeyed bread in Joseph's pleasant courtyard. His house, all clad in pristine white marble, reminded me of Caiaphas's palace, albeit a smaller version. Its imposing exterior belied the delicate beauty within. Unlike the Roman style, with its carefully embellished façades, the Hebrew way was to focus on the beauty of the living space.

Four divans were arranged around a long wooden table. Olive trees, shrubs, and potted flowers were placed strategically so as to create a contrast between the natural greenery and the patterned floral designs of the tapestried furniture.

I stared at our host and smiled. "You did not agree with Caiaphas and Annas." It was not a question. When he had come to me to ask for the body, his countenance had resembled that of a bereaved family member.

Looking over at Nicodemus, he nodded somberly. "We are two among his disciples. In an attempt to prevent this tragedy, we spent many exhausting hours arguing with Caiaphas and Annas and the rest of the Sanhedrin on behalf of Jesus—all to no avail."

I was curious about these men. Although fatigue was evident in the bruised shadows under their eyes, their expressions were vibrant. They were wary but did not seem afraid.

"There are others who feel the same, I gather." I recalled the many shocked and weeping faces among the Jews in the courtyard that excruciating Friday.

This time it was Nicodemus who spoke. "Yes, there are many."

The ensuing silence was comfortable. For the first time since I had been in this country, I did not feel separate...alien. Instead, I felt as relaxed as if I were sitting with fellow soldiers. Perhaps I was.

"Why...?" My voice was low, intentionally so, because these two wealthy, established men had quite clearly placed themselves at great risk within their community. Surely, those who had distorted the words and actions of Jesus and made him out to be a criminal would seek retribution against any who supported him or his memory. These crimes might in themselves be worthy of crucifixion. *Why would they risk losing their reputa-*

tions, perhaps livelihood, and even their lives by supporting Jesus?

"'Whoever has ears to hear ought to hear,'" chimed in Quintillus, as if quoting the dead king of the Jews was the most natural thing in the world for a Roman lead centurion. At the sharpness of my stare, he declared, "Lucius, this man Jesus spoke with *authority*. He raised the dead, healed the sick, and preached a subversive message—not against Caesar, but against oppression...injustice and war." Staring into his cup of tea and lowering his voice almost to a whisper, he continued, "'Forgive your enemies and bless those who curse you-who but the true son of God could say such a treasonous thing? Imagine, Lucius...a world without the endless bloodshed of boys fighting over contested boundaries...a world without invasions of peaceful lands on behalf of an ambitious emperor?"

This was not a conversation that should happen in front of strangers, I thought, just as Quintillus asked, "Do you think it a coincidence that he chose *this* place at *this* time?" His gaze roamed the room, pinned each of us in turn with its intensity. Then he turned back to me. "That Caesar is just a man, not the son of God, is not a revelation to you, me, or any legionnaire alive or dead." His eyes softened. "I know of your love for Tiberius. It is well-deserved. Clearly, he understood the gravity of that lie well enough to run away from his role as Princeps—twice. Unfortunately, he left behind a scoundrel to run the Empire."

Out of the corner of my eye, I saw our host and his friend edge upright against the cushions of their divans, intrigued by this surprising and powerful testimony of Quintillus.

I opened my mouth to speak, but my friend cut me off yet again.

"It was not by chance that Jesus chose *here* and *now* to present himself. There are far too many perfectly synchronized correlates, if one wants to *hear and see* them."

I let my awe at Quintillus's words wash over me. The air in the courtyard seemed to shimmer with the import of what he was implying. Was it my imagination, or did a new fragrance—something beyond that of the olive trees and flowers—envelop us as we sat? There was literally something in the air—subtle, unidentifiable, intoxicating.

The silence stretched on for several moments.

CHAPTER SIXTY-FOUR

Lucius Pontius Pilate

"Lucius, this last report that you want to make is not for Tiberius—or even for yourself." Quintillus stood suddenly and pivoted so that he could loom over me. Never had I seen tears standing in his eyes—even during our most horrific battles—yet his eyes glistened now. This warrior, the bravest man I had ever known, was crying for *me*.

"My friend," he continued, "you know full well who he is. You knew it as you stood beside him defending his life. Why else would you have argued Hebrew theology with Caiaphas and Annas and the rest of the Sanhedrin, just as our hosts had done the night before? No, this report is meant to serve another purpose. You want to record the supernatural—the miraculous— things you observed. You want to memorialize this god-man who condescended to be judged, found guilty, and crucified by the very men he came to save. Your compulsion arises from your own burning desire to leave a legacy of faith for those with ears to hear."

Breathing heavily, Quintillus stared at me for a long moment, as if to impress upon me the truth and weight of his words. And then he smiled, ignoring the tears that had overflowed and traced pathways down the planes of his face.

Is he correct? Is that why I linger in this place I have always hated? To make sure that I have left a legacy of...faith?

I thought back to those last moments I'd spent with the tortured, bleeding man. What leapt to mind was his unshakable confidence and nobility, but not just that. His *godliness*.

"You did not fail, my friend," Quintillus said, now attempting to cajole me. "You are not the one who crucified Jesus." He extended his arm and pointed toward Joseph and Nicodemus. "That is why you and I sit here with two of his disciples. They know you are one of them, although you do not yet know that."

Deeply touched, I felt the sting of tears in my own eyes. I opened my mouth to speak but found myself abruptly speechless, flustered.

Sensing my unease, Joseph stood to fill our cups with more tea, then came around the table to crouch between Quintillus and me. Gently, he took my right hand in his and then reached for Quintillus's left. "Brothers," he intoned. "You are no longer our enemies but our brothers." Then he gracefully stood to return to his seat. His silent friend smiled at him and very slightly nodded his head.

It felt as if we'd received a blessing.

Before I could respond, Joseph spoke again. "Nicodemus and I thank you for your eloquent and fervent profession of faith, my brother. A few of your observations are worthy of more discussion." He glanced again at Nicodemus, who was staring fixedly at Quintillus. Nicodemus bowed his head, in a gesture of reverence, lifted it, and said to Quintillus, "Your insight is remarkable. Clearly, it is God-given." Then he slowly turned back to regard Joseph and nodded, evidently communicating some type of affirmation or permission.

Turning back to me, Joseph asked, "May I call you Lucius?"

I laughed sardonically. "That is the only title I'll possess very shortly." I snorted. "Yes, of course."

We peered at each other unguardedly for a moment. Joseph did not appear much older than fifty—Quintillus's age. His head covering was unlike any I had ever seen: an elaborately braided, dark-brown headband over an embroidered cap of light tan. From under it emerged tufts of short, dark hair. He was clean-shaven, save a small beard at his chin, and wore a tunic of simple, light-tan linen that complemented his head covering. Without the hat, this attractive man might have passed for an affluent Greek or Roman.

His friend Nicodemus looked twenty years older and wore the heavy facial hair, headdress, and robe that I had become accustomed to seeing on Hebrew men. The two seemed as unlikely a pair as Quintillus and I.

Joseph leaned forward, his expression keen. "I would like to answer your 'why' of earlier, Lucius. Your friend is quite right. You did not crucify Jesus; his death was prophesied. But, before saying more on that matter, your use of those words *subversive* and *treasonous* when speaking about Jesus, Quintillus, gives me pause." He leaned back and gazed in the direction of the centurion, his expression pensive. In the still courtyard, the call of a mourning dove echoed in the stillness. "My brother," he continued, "can you explain your argument to Annas, Caiaphas, and the rest of the Sanhedrin last Friday night?"

Nicodemus seemed taken aback—shocked. Quite clearly, he did not expect his friend to speak of this matter, and his thick, white eyebrows met at the start of a frown. *Brother? Are you so certain of this, Joseph?* Very deliberately, he placed his cup of tea on the table and exhaled. Then, glancing quickly at Joseph, the elder stared directly at me for a long moment and then at Quintillus once again. He looked like a scholar. I could see his eyes—dark gray with deep indentations at the corners from years of squinting at scrolls of Mosaic law—moisten as he addressed me, his voice quavering with emotion.

"We have always employed the same logic as you, Lucius...one we call *pagan*." His expression revealed his understanding of the irony of his statement. "Moses did indeed prophesy a man 'like one of us,' whose every word was truth and every action God's; one who would heal the sick, raise the dead, reassemble the lost tribes of Israel, and establish the kingdom of God. The protests of the High Priests were easily refuted—just as you refuted them—because they were nonsense."

He coughed in an attempt to clear his voice of its emotional thickening. The heavily veined hand that had held the tea came up to support his jaw. As he buried it in his thick white beard, only the tips of his fingers were visible. "This man's miraculous abilities were not demonic, everyone there knew this—all seventy-one members of the Sanhedrin. Annas and Caiaphas best of all." His voice caught, and he coughed again, cleared his throat. "Caiaphas—may God have mercy on his soul—insisted, that it was better for one man to die than a whole nation. Only four of us dared oppose him. It was Annas who ruled that we take a vote."

Nicodemus lowered his head for a moment, blinking rapidly. Then he turned to Quintillus, his dark-gray gaze electrifying. "*Treasonous* and *subversive* indeed, my new brother. Of all the prophets who have arisen in Israel, Jesus was the first to call himself the son of God. He was the first to say he would show us his Father. *Our* Father. He promised to help us *see* what we had done in accepting the Ten Commandments and ignoring the Father's prohibition to add to them." His voice now cracked with emotion and weariness, and his expression turned scornful. "Oh, but how we added to them, Quintillus! Jesus preached that we reduce our 615 impossible rules to two: *Love your God with your whole soul, mind, and heart; and love your neighbor as yourself.* This liberation from the law was an open invitation to divinity. Many people saw who he was. And, yes, they wept."

He peered at Quintillus. "I had not considered why the Lord chose this moment to make himself manifest in the world. After hundreds of years, why now? Your observations are more than remarkable; they are the *truth.* My friend, "he continued, "I had not considered your question before...*Do you think it a co-incidence that he chose this place at this time?*" Blinking rapidly again, but now with excitement and vitality, he said, "The statement you made to Lucius about your view of the Roman Emperor, 'that Caesar is just a man, not the son of God, is not a revelation,' you said. 'To you, me, or any legionnaire alive or dead!'" Nicodemus's face radiated light as he proclaimed, "This time has been foreordained from the beginning of Creation!"

Tipping his face heavenward, the elder continued, "Thy mystery is inexhaustible. Why you chose to let Joseph and me *see* and everyone else remain blind is incomprehensible to me, but I thank you for the sight. For the sight you gave these men."

Nicodemus then turned to me. "Last week, when Jesus destroyed the animal stalls and drove the vendors and money-changers from outside the Temple, his open hostility toward the commerce of the Temple ignited a flame. Do you think for one moment that he could not have stopped all of this had he chosen to do so?" His tone grew reverential. "The Lord and master of the universe, he who created Annas, Caiaphas, and each of us, offered himself to the Father. Willingly. In the land of the people whom God had led out of Egypt, he came to teach us that love trumps the law—always and forever." A heavy and tremulous sigh escaped him as he concluded, "But the same tired sins blinded us to his divinity: jealousy, pride, and greed."

We four sat for many hours as Nicodemus continued speaking. He told us how a young boy of around twelve had appeared in the Temple close to twenty years before. The boy was from Bethlehem and even then, spoke with authority.

When Nicodemus rested, Joseph told of the evening he'd spent in the tomb with Mary, the mother of that boy grown to manhood, and of Mary's extraordinary story about his conception and birth, their subsequent flight into Egypt, and their return to Judea once Herod the Great had died and the way was safe.

Jesus's words washed over me: *You would have no power over me if it had not been given to you from above. For this reason, the one who handed me over to you has the greater sin.*

CHAPTER SIXTY-FIVE

Claudia Procula

Quintillus stood in the doorway of my chambers. "Lucius asked that I take care of you," he said gravely.

I was standing next to Antonia, who had been crying more or less steadily since the day that seemed never to have ended. She had never left my side, not once, though there were a few times when I had almost begged her to leave me alone. The pain in her eyes had stilled the words in my throat. Antonia had been like my mother to me throughout my life. Taking out my frustration on her would be unforgivable.

Quintillus was formal, his scarlet uniform resplendent. "Is he...?"

He shook his head, quickly, sharply. I wasn't to ask. Not then.

It had been almost four weeks since Jesus had been crucified, and I had not seen or heard from Lucius in all that time. As I stood staring at his closest confidant, I thought about the seemingly endless days I had spent waiting for my husband. And I thought about the day I saw the mother of the righteous one once again.

A week earlier, I had persuaded Antonia and Gracian to accompany me to the market. It had been over three weeks since I had stepped outside the palace, and neither could refuse my entreaties.

Avoiding the Upper City seemed prudent; we would be less likely to see the priests or temple guards. Naively hoping to distract myself with some shopping, we made our way down the Lower City's narrow dark streets, past its small, dark houses. Dressed in outer robes and hoods, Antonia and I easily blended in with the Hebrew women at the market—and Gracian looked like any other legionnaire.

While feigning interest in some figs, I felt a soft nudge. I turned and found myself facing the woman whom I had knelt to help collect the blood of her son. The gentleness in her face astounded me, and the tenderness in her penetrating eyes seared my soul. Without thinking, I extended my hand to her. She grabbed it and pulled me close with surprising strength. Her hair was covered by her tunic, but the garment was diaphanous enough to reveal the lovely blue of the stole underneath, as well as her lustrous, dark hair. At her touch, I felt the precise shimmer that always presaged one of my inner journeys to Delphi. Her arresting face once again transformed into that of the Oracle, but this time in a younger guise.

We said nothing—what words could possibly express what we had shared?—but the influx of perception, wisdom, love, and tenderness stretched my being until I felt I could contain no more.

I blinked, and she was gone. I was standing, staring at the place where she had stood when Antonia approached and asked if I was ready to return to the palace. Her baskets were loaded with fresh fruits and vegetables.

Our hearts are such fragile, tender things. Even when we are told exactly what is to come, and we experience it as if it were occurring in real time, when the worst thing comes, we play a game.

I had been told from the start that Lucius and I would have just five years together, but at fifteen, five years sounds like a very long time—a third of one's life. Now, a few months before my twenty-first birthday, it seemed like just an instant. The knowledge that I would never again experience his embrace, feel his kisses, make love with him, lay like a massive boulder on my heart that was getting heavier by the second. How could I take my next breath? And yet I did. And I would…again and again… many hundreds of thousands of times.

Quintillus stood silently as I collected myself. "Where are we to go?" I asked, finally.

"Your uncle Adrian will meet us in Athens."

"Us?" I was surprised at the thought that Quintillus might leave Jerusalem. That meant that Lucius…I did not allow myself to complete the thought lest I collapse.

He nodded.

"When do we leave?"

Quintillus looked over my shoulder at the hideously bright early-morning spring sun.

"Noon."

CHAPTER SIXTY-SIX

THE MEDITERRANEAN SEA, EAST OF CRETA
Claudia Procula

By the time we were just a few days from Athens, I had read the *Final Report of Lucius Pontius Pilate to Tiberius Caesar on the Crucifixion of the Christ* five times over. Written in my husband's precise script, the work was—paradoxically—both methodical and random in its observations. Lucius had begun writing it in the style of the adjutant, recording the events of the week leading up to the crucifixion and his own attempts to inject reason and truth into the proceedings. The objectivity with which he wrote about the culminating day both broke my heart and made it swell with pride—at his courage, character, and clarity of thinking.

The remainder of the text was an amalgam of testimony from people I mostly did not know. These included a man called Nicodemus and another called Joseph. Their commentary and those of others featured graphic descriptions of various miracles wrought by Jesus—including the multiplication of bread and fish and a number of healings—along with portions of his teachings. At one point, Quintillus himself was quoted:

I had been following a huge crowd of people. The scene looked like one that could readily degenerate into chaos, and so I drew close—close enough to watch a woman approach Jesus. She fell at his feet as she touched a portion of his robe. Instantly he stopped and shouted, "Who touched me?"

Several of his disciples were as astounded as I. There were hordes of people in front, in back, and to his sides, and yet he wanted to know who had touched him?

Because Jesus had stopped still, the crowd parted, and the woman lying at his feet was safe from being trampled by people pushing and shoving to get close to him. As I looked down on the prone woman from astride my horse, I wondered about the depth of desperation required to risk being trampled. And I thought of my servant, Marius, whose illness had progressed beyond the skills of my medic Gracian. He was dying.

I heard Jesus say, "I felt the power go out of me," just as he saw the woman. He leaned down to grab both of her hands and said, "Your faith has healed you."

Before I could stop myself, I jumped to the ground and strode up to Jesus. His disciples looked annoyed, but he looked merely curious, ignoring his followers as he waited for me. I, a Roman soldier, was intent on begging for his intervention for Marius.

Standing in front of him, looking into his face, I was astonished at my own great belief that this man—who resembled all others but spoke like no other—could heal Marius.

"Lord, one of my servants is dying. He is grievously tormented."

His reply was instantaneous. "I will come and heal him. Show me where he lays."

Shocked, I thought, *I cannot bring him into a Roman soldier's barracks! "Lord," I said, "I am not worthy that you should come under my roof. But speak the word only, and my servant shall be healed. Like you, Sir, I am a man with authority. I have hundreds of soldiers under me. I say to this man, 'Go,' and he goes; and to another, 'Come,' and he comes; and to my servant, 'Do this,' and he does it."*

Jesus looked surprised...and pleased. "Then go your way," he said. "And as you have believed, so will it be done."

I was unsurprised when I got back to the barracks and found Marius sitting up and drinking tea. From that moment, he had been healed.

"Claudia, you will wear out his writing if you read the report another time."

I had not heard Quintillus enter my chamber. He was smiling, for he could see the section I was reading again and again. His own words.

He stood clothed in a simple white toga, the kind Lucius used to wear. I returned his smile, aware that I had not done such a thing in a very long time.

"Would you ladies like to walk up to the deck with me? It's a glorious afternoon, and I think both of you could use some ocean air."

"No, thank you, Quintillus," said Antonia. "You and

Claudia go on ahead. I am not feeling all that well...the motion of the ship...."

Indeed, Antonia had a peculiar look on her face—but I can't say she looked ill. More like...*expectant*? I brushed off the thought and went to grab my cloak.

CHAPTER SIXTY-SEVEN

"You were right, Quintillus, thank you for suggesting a walk. The air is beautiful, intoxicating. I am delightfully chilly for the first time in years!" I had to shout to be heard above the sound of the wind. I had forgotten how life-affirming a sea breeze could be. I felt washed clean as I stood next to Lucius's best friend, my hair blowing wildly around my face. I hugged my robe tight to my body to keep it from blowing away. For the first time, I thought of my five-year union with intense gratitude instead of crushing despair at its brevity. I knew at that moment that I would once again feel joy.

I could see the outline of Creta to the west. We would be in Athens very soon...*home.* There was a time when my heart would have soared at the thought, but at that moment it sank, and I brought my clenched hand to my mouth to mitigate the painful twisting of my insides. *Athens is not my home. It never was. My home is gone. Returning to live with Uncle Adrian and Aunt Sabina...how can I possibly do this? Am I to pretend that I have never been a wife and mother...forget about each of the baby boys I conceived and named, though none lived past four months in my womb? My aunt and uncle will have questions. Of course, they will want to know what has happened in my life. Five years of happenings. And of course, they will wonder about Lucius. What happened to him? They will want to discuss all the details...What was all that uproar among the Jews?...*

I sensed Quintillus watching me. Blinking rapidly, I bit my knuckle hard and thought, *After all this, I cannot cry—not in front of him!* I took a deep breath and turned to him, relieved when he took me into his arms and murmured something I could not hear. How good it felt to be held, if only for a few moments.

"Let's get you some hot tea, you are shivering," he said, his lips close to my ear so that I could hear him over the roar of the wind. His grip around my waist was strong as he guided me along the deck of the ship, which was now plunging up and into good-sized waves in the increasingly turbulent sea.

Sitting in the nearly empty dining hall, I wrapped my hands about the mug of hot tea and looked across at Quintillus—really looked at him—aware that I had rarely done so...Lucius had so suffused my vision for the past five years.

His almost black hair was shot through with gray, curly tendrils that clung to his high forehead. His eyes, almond-shaped, were a warm brown with amber flecks.

Why...he is quite handsome.

"Do you *want* to return to the home of Adrian and Sabina, Claudia?" he asked gravely. Although his gaze never left mine, Quintillus looked discomfited. His dark olive skin was flushed.

"What do you mean?"

The end of his mouth curled up. "I am asking if going back to the home of your aunt and uncle pleases you."

"Pleases me?" *What is he talking about?*

Exasperated, Quintillus growled, the nostrils of his long Roman nose flaring. "Claudia, would you like to marry me?"

Into my shocked silence, he said in a softer tone. "Claudia...Lucius asked that I take care of you if he could not. I promised him that I would. If we are together, we can live in a place where you are not known as the wife of Lucius Pontius Pilate. You can avoid the interminable questions about what happened in Jerusalem on that Friday. And on that early Sunday morning. And besides that, I think...perhaps...we might find some measure of happiness in each other's company."

Finally, I cried. All the sobs that I had been holding back escaped in torrents. Desperately, I tried to speak my *yes* into the gasps. He seemed to understand and, when I had finally collected myself to look up into his amber eyes, he smiled broadly.

CHAPTER SIXTY-EIGHT

ON SHIP SAILING TO ATHENS
Claudia Procula

Three days later, Quintillus and I were married on the ship. Antonia had somewhere learned enough about Roman wedding custom that she directed me to wear a white tunic with a knotted woolen belt. Suspecting that her source was either Zahra or Sabu, I had smiled to myself as she fussed over the knot, thinking of another wedding a lifetime ago. Antonia was even able to fashion a *flammeum*, the deep-yellow wedding veil of the Roman bride. She'd never admitted that she and Quintillus had spoken about his proposal long before he made it, but I was certain they had done so.

Ignoring our protests, she spoke with the captain, who decided that the wedding would be a nice excuse for a celebration. He even made an unscheduled landing on Creta so that the newlyweds could enjoy their wedding night on land.

When the ship docked in Athens, Uncle Adrian was there alone to meet us. I'd worried a little at the reception Quintillus and I would receive, but was relieved to find that my uncle readily accepted the presence of Quintillus as my new husband. To my surprise, he also appeared relieved. As a member of the Greek Agora, I knew that Uncle Adrian had heard about the calamitous events in Judea...and of the fate of Lucius. There was sadness in his eyes when he greeted me and his smiles remained on his lips. I wondered at that but was grateful that he asked no questions of Quintillus or me.

I wondered if Sabina would feel the same as he—and why she hadn't accompanied him. Their house was not far from the harbor, after all. But, following my uncle's lead, I decided to keep the question to myself.

"Claudia...I wonder if we might take some time to stop for a drink at the tavern just half a short way down the street?" Adrian followed my gaze toward the many bags lying on the cement nearby and understood my concern. He signaled to a nearby sailor, and as the man approached, said, "Sir, here is two drachmas. Would you please watch these bags for my niece and her fellow travelers? We'll not be more than ninety minutes or so." He pointed over at the long building across the street.

Though it was just a little past two in the afternoon, the tavern was filled with sailors drinking and eating. Somehow, we found a table and Adrian ordered for the four of us. He waited until each of us had sampled the hummus, pita, bits of fish, and wine before speaking. *The last five years had not been kind to him*, I thought. The sadness in his eyes intensified as he studied us.

"You both look beautiful," he said, directing his gaze first at Antonia and then at me. "The years in the desert have been good for you." Turning to Quintillus, he said, "You were at that chariot race where I met Lucius. You were a legionnaire also, as I recall...a centurion."

Quintillus's eyes widened as he nodded. "You have an excellent memory, sir."

Pleasantries over, Adrian's expression darkened, and his

eyes filled with profound pain. "Claudia…there's something I must tell you—or perhaps you have gathered it from her absence. Your aunt died last month."

About to eat a fig, I placed it back on my plate, suddenly nauseous. *Sabina…all that earthy vitality…and Lucius, the most vibrant man I have ever known. So much loss—how is one to bear it?*

I regarded my uncle through eyes quickly filling with tears. "I cannot tell you how very sorry I am, Uncle. Was it sudden?"

Clearly working hard to maintain control of his emotions, Adrian nodded. He took a long draught of wine, swallowed, and said, "She developed a fever. Very high. The doctor could not get it down. She experienced convulsions and died. It all happened in less than forty-eight hours and, honestly, the household is still in shock." He looked dazed as he gripped the table's edge so hard his knuckles whitened.

I well understood his pain.

He stared at me for a long moment. "We have both been through a great deal in recent weeks, my child." His voice lowered to a whisper and his eyes glistened. "I cannot imagine the horrors you have witnessed, Claudia…and the strength required of you to bear it all, my child of wisdom."

A collage of conflicting thoughts and emotions flashed through my mind and heart. I owed this man my life. He had taken me in, taught me to love learning and to understand and respect the greatest thinkers of our time. Now he needed help, while I was safe and protected. I felt an obligation to do something.

My uncle must have read my mind. Leaning forward across the table, he grabbed one of Quintillus's hands and one of my own and placed them one on top of the other. Tears stood in his eyes. "I want you to know that…in spite of all that has happened, I am so very happy for you both. I offer my heartfelt congratulations and very best wishes."

On impulse, I brought out the container that held the dowry I had left with a lifetime ago. Before leaving the ship, I had explained to Quintillus that I planned to return it to my aunt and uncle. Quintillus had thought it an excellent idea.

Placing it on the table, I said, "Uncle..." My voice cracked with emotion, and I coughed in an attempt to disguise it and moved on. "Lucius gave this to Quintillus for safekeeping on the day he left for—"

"Child, that is your gift. I do not want it back. Please. I want for nothing. You and Quintillus must use it for whatever you'd like."

I was grateful that he'd interrupted me before I'd had to utter anything about Rome, and Lucius's fate by his own hand. Although Quintillus had never spoken it, I knew he had waited until Lucius had left for Rome to come and collect Antonia and me, and that he understood—just as I did—what would happen to my husband after that. I knew that he had waited through the time it would take Lucius to get to the palace of the Emperor and receive Sejanus's final and most villainous proclamation: "You have dishonored the Empire. You must take your own life!"

I had been told by the Oracle that Lucius would die by his own hand before he was forty. Mercifully, she had not told me how or where or precisely when it would happen.

CHAPTER SIXTY-NINE

Claudia Procula

"Claudia, come quickly! I don't know how long he will be there. Our horses are saddled..." Quintillus raced into the kitchen where we were preparing food for Uncle Adrian and his new wife; Sabu and his wife, Zahra; and Gracian—all of whom were scheduled to arrive within the next few days.

Surveying the long tables filled with a variety of foods in preparation, and at the five women working hard to complete them, Quintillus implored, "Antonia, can you get along without my wife for tonight if I promise to get her back here by this time tomorrow? This surprise I have in store for her will not wait much longer."

She smiled broadly. Antonia had loved Quintillus from the moment she'd met him back in Caesarea. There was a time when I'd hoped they would marry, back during my idyllic days with Lucius.

"Of course! Go, Claudia." She darted a look at Demeter, Penelope, and Naomi, all of whom were engrossed in baking bread, preparing lentils, and dressing the lamb Quintillus had slaughtered that morning. She nodded, satisfied at their progress. "None of our guests will arrive for at least three more days, so no need to hurry!" But Quintillus had already left to tend the waiting horses.

I gave Antonia a quick hug, whispered a "thank you so much," and hurried out to join my husband.

As we rode southwest, I pondered how quickly the years had rolled by. Almost ten years ago to the day, we had purchased this working farm from an elderly Greek widow. Her one request of us was that we keep the three servants who had maintained the olive and fruit trees and produced sufficient corn and vegetable crops to provide a comfortable living. Since Antonia and I had only a rudimentary knowledge of farming and Quintillus had none, we happily included Demeter, Penelope, and Naomi into our fold.

Quintillus was receiving a generous retirement pension from Rome and had saved most of his salary for the previous twenty-five years. This money, along with my dowry, was enough to meet the widow's steep price and take care of our on-going expenses.

After two hours of hard riding, I realized where we were going—and it alarmed me. I could see now that Quintillus was heading in the direction of the Sacred Springs, the Agora, and the Christian settlement of Aquila and his wife, Priscilla. I prodded my horse Aurora with both knees, and in minutes, was keeping pace with Quintillus and his stallion. At my motion to slow down, Quintillus did so, though his expression darkened.

"I cannot go to their camp, Quintillus. Not after what happened last year. Please..."

"We will be lost in the crowd," he replied, his expression softening as he recalled what had happened when, against my better judgment, Antonia and I traveled to the Sacred Spring to "seek the company of others who might have known the Christ," as she had phrased it.

"That's what I thought last year, Quintillus. But a woman recognized me and began to shout, 'Look! That's Pontius Pilate's wife over there!' Soon, Antonia and I were surrounded by a screaming mob...their faces were just like those in my dreams. 'Why didn't you stop him! Why didn't you stop your husband from crucifying our Lord?!'"

As I recalled the scene, dread and fear began to enshroud me. I was close to tears. Suddenly, Quintillus plucked me off of Aurora and gently placed me on the ground next to him. He enfolded me in his arms as our horses wandered off to enjoy the sweet grass of the fertile valley. Although he was over sixty, my husband looked and moved like a far younger man; the only sign of his age was the broadening shock of white that ran through the black hair at his temple. His face remained smooth and youthful, his body muscular and lean, thanks to his years as a legionnaire and the strenuous physical labor of working the farm.

"Claudia," he whispered confidently into my ear, "I promise you there will be no repeat of that ignorant cruelty from the Christians."

Enfolded in his embrace, I calmed instantly. "I believe you," I murmured into his broad neck. "Whatever you are taking me to see, it must be very important to you. I imagine we'd better make haste, though, since you said there was not much time."

CHAPTER SEVENTY

SACRED SPRING SANCTUARY, CORINTH, GREECE
Claudia Procula

"The Jews demand a sign and the Greeks look for wisdom. Your prayer and inscription on this shrine, *To an Unknown God,* show your hunger for the truth of the One True God."

At my sharp inhalation of breath, Quintillus clasped my hand hard. The crowd was indeed huge, as Quintillus had predicted, but no one noticed the man and woman edging toward the back of the throng. They were wholly caught up in the testimony of this former Pharisee, Saul of Tarsus, as he recounted the story of his persecution of Christians and his extraordinary conversion to preaching "the gospel of the Christ." He had later changed his name to Paul.

My heart soared and raced at the memory of that shrine to an unknown God. And of Lucius.

Quintillus and I had lived in our new home for just two weeks when he told me that he must return to Rome and that he would be gone for some months. I knew the trip had something to do with Lucius. He knew that I knew, but in that strangely effective way that men and women have of communicating wordlessly, we felt no need to discuss it. To do so seemed irrelevant—perhaps even harmful. Upon his return, several months later, we made the journey to Corinth, to the Sacred Spring. Although I had never before been there, I had heard of the place from Sabina, who had stopped there on her way to the Temple of Artemis and Apollo. There had been no Christian encampment then. Perhaps the word *Christian* had not yet even been uttered.

It was late spring when my new husband and I made the journey, and the valley was still lush and green, dotted with wildflowers of all colors. The effect was a vivid tapestry that seemed miraculous after the arid, rocky limestone land we had just traversed.

I could not deny the beauty of the Temple to Artemis and Apollo. Its uniquely pleasing Greek architecture was evident in the gigantic curving columns that seemed to reach to the heavens.

Quintillus pointed to a gigantic shrine crowned by the words, *To an Unknown God.* It overlooked one of the two rivers that poured into the Sacred Spring. The stone was beautiful, rainbow-hued marble that the setting sun had lit on fire.

"Lucius." It was little more than a breath, but Quintillus nodded. This stunning spot was my late husband's burial place, his grave marked by a simple and profound testament to the God he had tried so hard to defend.

I knew there could be no monument naming him. Any identification of the Governor of Judea would invite desecration of the worst sort.

Brought back to the present by this man called Paul, I heard him say, "We have not received the spirit of the world but the spirit who is from God, so that we may understand the things freely given us from God. And we speak about them not with words taught by human wisdom, but with words taught by the Spirit, describing spiritual realities in spiritual terms.

"Now, the natural man does not accept what pertains to the Spirit of God, for to him it is foolishness, and he cannot understand it because it is judged spiritually. The one who is spiritual, however, can judge everything but is not subject to judgment by anyone.

"For 'who has known the mind of the Lord, so as to counsel him?' But we have the mind of Christ."

Although the crowd of people gathered to listen was vast and continued to grow after we arrived, there was no sound to compete with Paul's message. Even the many children in the arms of their mothers were quiet. I reached for Quintillus's hand, and as I did so, I sensed someone's eyes upon me. Looking around, I saw her. She stood near the portico of the Temple of Artemis and Apollo, dressed precisely as she had been that last time I had seen her at the market in Jerusalem. The light-blue robe covered her slim shape, and a diaphanous tunic was pulled up to partially cover her dark hair. Her smile felt like a blessing.

Turning his gaze to look at the mother of Christ, Quintillus smiled, first at her, then at me. "We should go now, Claudia. We want to be home when our guests arrive."

EPILOGUE

Delphi
Claudia Procula

Am I a Christian?

Even now, after almost eighty years of existence, as I approach my life's end, I do not know how to answer that question. This is primarily because the word seems too small. How can such a simple word stand for something that defies description or definition?

Logos. The Word.

My inability to identify myself as *Christian* was ever a source of consternation for my dear Antonia, who feared for my soul. Even on her deathbed, when she was older than I am now—eighty-five—she could not rest because I had not committed. She spent much of her dwindling strength pleading with me to join the local Christian group in Corinth that she had helped start.

My reluctance had nothing whatsoever to do with my faith in *Logos*. I tried and failed on countless occasions to explain to my friend why I could not join her group. Somehow, I could never get past the vocabulary: *savior, soul, eternal life, baptism, repentance...*

But that is sophistry, and I admit it readily. I attended the very first meeting with Antonia, confident that I would join. That was before I was identified as the wife of Lucius. But, almost from the start, I felt an aversion to the certitude of the husband-and-wife group leaders, Aquila and Priscilla. There seemed to be a tautology in their answers to my long list of questions.

"What is it to be Christian?" I asked.

"To follow Christ."

"How do I follow someone I cannot see?"

"You see him with the eyes of your faith."

"What is faith?"

"To know that Jesus Christ died for you and for me and that on the third day, he ascended into heaven."

The answers felt rote, mechanical.

To this day, I do not know if my early and ongoing immersion in Plato and Socrates, Heraclitus, Epictetus, Pythagoras, and the other Greek philosophers was a burden or a blessing for my soul. Nor do I know if I have benefited from the knowledge, visions, and prescience bestowed on me by the Oracle. It has never seemed sensible to ask this question. I only mention it now because soon my ability to do so will be at an end. My tongue and pen will soon be silenced, so it seems important to attempt an explanation of my decisions and motives.

I use the word *attempt* quite deliberately: I know that I can never fully reveal the essence of my meaning, but I hope I can get close enough that you might hear its echo. The truth always resides outside the boundaries of our words...just outside our reach. Long ago, I accepted that our view of what *is* remains delimited by our language, experience, preconceptions, and many other factors within and outside of our control.

The greatest privilege of my life was to be the wife of Lucius. Although we were together for just five years, our love was deeper and more immense than the heavens on view here in Delphi. I say this not to demean the years I lived as the wife of

Quintullus. Those were years of peace and contentment for us both. Our work on our farm together, my tutoring of young women in the thoughts and words of my mentors, all of this was fulfilling and brought us sustenance and joy.

Like all legionary soldiers, Quintillus had remained unmarried until he took me as his wife at age fifty-two. I was strangely unsurprised when he proposed marriage, and relieved and grateful beyond words. We had always shared a bond, Quintillus and I. Each of us had loved Lucius as we had no other human being, so there could never be any suggestion of jealousy or guilt for either of us. More than that—Lucius had asked Quintillus to take care of me if the worst came to pass, and it was his gift to his friend to do so.

Although I was just twenty-one when Quintillus and I married, I never again conceived. This was as the Oracle had predicted. Was I disappointed? Yes and no. *Yes,* because, like all women, my body hungered to partner with the Creator and bring forth life. And *no,* because the faces of my three precious boys would remain inscribed on my heart and soul to this day, more than five decades after their deaths.

After Quintillus died, I sold our farm and moved back here, to Delphi. As the daughter of Aurora, I was asked by the women of the shrine to become the Oracle—but I was compelled to decline. I had looked into the countenance of the last Oracle, and I knew that any who might come after her would be but a simulacrum.

AFTERWORD

The decision to write *I, Claudia* created that oxymoronic combination of emotions—terror and unbridled excitement—and that is exactly what assured me it was worthwhile. I felt these things not just because historical fiction is a genre wholly new to me, but because Pontius Pilate is real: he lived, breathed, hoped, and dreamed...but is forever trapped in the pages of history.

Pilate is a man with whom I began to feel a powerful affinity once I started praying the prayers of the Catholic Church. Not only could I sympathize with his awful dilemma, I felt that I could "stand under" it, having faced my own. When Pilate was confronted with an impossible choice, he was wholly clear on the right action to take—and what was at stake if he didn't—yet he was entirely incapable of bringing it to fruition. In his case, this was because of an oath. In my own, it was because of a promise.

More daunting than my fear of trying something new was the awe of writing about the crucifixion of Christ! Just how does one approach such a task? Precisely, it turns out, the same way as any other: begin.

Long before I converted to Catholic Christianity, before I had any notion that I would do so, I discovered Elaine Pagels' *The Gnostic Gospels*. Among the countless things I came to understand from my careful reading of this splendid book was Pagels' breakdown of the word *history*.

To paraphrase from her afterword, history—*his-story*—is written by the winners. That simply worded thought flattened me. Everything we write is biased—or prejudiced, if you prefer—by the experience and viewpoint of the author. That includes history, which we tend to think of as synonymous with *truth*.

Of course! Why didn't I know this years ago?

Just so, the entire life and character of the man called

Pontius Pilate have been ossified by four words in the Apostles' Creed: "crucified under Pontius Pilate." The Creed defines the Christian faith and has been prayed by believers for centuries. I wanted to break through the crypt those words have put him in to create a person we could see, feel, and hear despite the passage of more than 2,000 years.

My account of the crucifixion is based upon the Gospels of John and Nicodemus. Of the four synoptic Gospels, only John extends Pilate's interrogation into a series of four increasingly intense and desperate attempts to thwart the High Priests. This interrogation lasted several hours, consuming much of that Friday morning in April. Scholars agree that John's Gospel was written close to the end of the first century, and reason suggests it is the more accurate. Perhaps it was even inspired by the Spirit. Nicodemus's account is unabashedly laudatory of Pilate's efforts to stop the High Priests.

There is no doubt that a man called Lucius Pontius Pilate lived and was the Governor of Judea from approximately 26 through 36 AD. Other matters are not as clear. He did have a military background, but chariot racing may or may not have been his passion. Seneca may or may not have been his friend. Four countries claim to be the place where he was buried, and Greece is not among them. In bringing him—and especially his bride—to life, I was moved to allow my imagination to embroider upon what I studied.

Claudia Procula is mentioned only in the Gospel of Mark. Since none of the others mention her, some scholars believe she did not exist. Others insist that she would not have been at the Jerusalem Temple during the Jewish Passover, as it would have been far too dangerous there for a woman. But her admonition to her husband in Mark's Gospel is, at the very least, evocative. "Have nothing to do with that righteous man....".

From the moment I began to conceive of this book, Claudia was Greek—a Delphine. Like anyone who has had the privilege of visiting Delphi, I found the place haunting and holy. There is mysticism in each pebble and echoes of the Oracles in the ruins of the temples. On a journey there alone, I could literally hear the whispered prayers of the ages as I made my way down through the crumbling ruins of the shrine. It is a sacred place. Claudia Procula could have been from no other place on earth.

Giving Claudia a bit of a philosophical bent provided me with an excuse to revisit friends from a time when I believed in nothing. If I overdid my citations of the great ancient thinkers, please forgive the excess.

That Lucius Pontius Pilate has emerged as such a sympathetic character in this story may confound, even annoy or madden some readers. Perhaps that is not such a bad thing.

Including Delphi, each of the cities mentioned in the story appears on maps of the ancient Roman Empire. My description of King Herod's architectural genius, made manifest in Caesarea and Jerusalem, is, if anything, understated. It is difficult to do justice to the brilliance of this man before he fell victim to his apparently insatiable appetites. And many of the more surprising details are absolutely real: in the Caesarean palace where Pilate lived, for example, there was indeed a freshwater swimming pool.

That Pontius Pilate built an aqueduct to the Jerusalem Temple is a matter of record, as is the riot that erupted after Caiaphas accused Pilate of using Temple funds to finance it. The uprising caused the deaths of many more than the four Judeans I focus on. (For this story, I moved the riot from Jerusalem to Caesarea.)

The architecture, culture, dress, foods, and modes of travel I describe are based on the descriptions in historical sources.

Although this was not a book I had planned to write, I am entirely grateful for the inspiration. Each time I recited the

Creed or prayed the Sorrowful Mysteries of the Rosary, I thought about this man, Pilate; about his suffering. Because, surely, he did suffer. I continually wondered what I would have done if placed in his situation—an alien asked to do the impossible. Most frequently, I wondered what it must have felt like to stand next to Christ. I hope I did Lucius justice.

Not long after my conversion to Catholicism, my then spiritual director, Father Paul McCollum, introduced me to the work of the brilliant theologian Karl Rahner. Father Paul and I had been discussing the long list of reasons that had impelled me to walk away from God as a young woman and spend many years opposed to religion and all that it represents. The "exclusivity" of Christianity had been among my top complaints. When he'd heard this, the priest had smiled and said, "You need to read Rahner." He immediately lent me a textbook he had used while in the seminary.

It is Karl Rahner who coined the phrase "anonymous Christian" to describe men and women of "good will" who have not been catechized. Rahner's categorization provided the solution to a problem that had plagued me for much of my life. Whether because of culture or ethnicity, these are people who have never encountered the Gospel, but who, through some mysterious and unknown power known only to Christ, merit salvation. A middle way, if you will. Plodding through the dense writing of the theologian, I found a new "friend"—just as the priest had predicted. One who lives outside of the absolutism of damnation and salvation.

The phrase *anonymous Christian* describes men and women like Lucius, Claudia, and Quintillus: people who follow their conscience and live lives of redemptive faith, not mere belief. Rahner's own words express it best: "In every human person...there is something like an anonymous, unthematic, perhaps repressed, basic experience of being oriented to God...which can be repressed but not destroyed, which is 'mystical' or (if you prefer a more cautious terminology) has its climax in what the classical masters called infused contemplation."

ACKNOWLEDGMENTS

For readers intrigued enough by the places and people of this story to want to learn more, I recommend several books. Although reading about Delphi is but a poor substitute for experiencing it, William J. Broad's *The Oracle* (Penguin Press, New York, New York, 2000) offers comprehensive history and archaeology. Michael Scott's *Delphi: A History of the Center of the World* (Princeton University Press, Princeton, New Jersey 2014) provides intriguing descriptions of the Oracles and spectacular photographs. In *The Road to Delphi* (Farrar, Straus, and Giroux, New York, New York, 2003), Michel Wood offers an intriguing and thoughtful history of the Oracles themselves.

For the background on ancient Israel and Rome and their cultures, *Ben Hur: A Tale of the Christ* by Carol Wallace (Tyndale House Publishers, Carol Stream, Illinois, 2016) was invaluable.

The list of sources for material about Pontius Pilate is nothing less than daunting. At the top of my nonfiction list are three. In *Pontius Pilate* by Anne Wroe (Random House, New York, 1999), the author's scope of research is astounding. Aldo Schiavone's *Pontius Pilate* (Liveright Publishing, New York, 2016) is a rare attempt at an unbiased, historically accurate view of the Prelate of Judea. And *What Do We Know About Pontius Pilate?* by Simon Webb (Langley Press, Durham, NC 2018) offers a quick overview of Pilate and the crucifixion, mainly through the lens of the three canonical gospels. *Pontius Pilate: A Novel* by Paul L. Maier (Kregel Publications, Grand Rapids Michigan, 1968) was useful because Maier grounds his story in extensive, and mostly historically accurate research.

There is far less information available about Claudia. Although I found some eight novels about her, they served mainly to tell me who she was *not*. The sole exception was a 1959 novel by Esther Kellner (Appleton–Century–Croft, New York). Her

Claudia was finely drawn and the ancient background vivid but not overdone.

The Letters of Pontius Pilate (WP Crozier, J.H. Sears & Co., New York, 1928) are evidently apocryphal, but I relied on them more than a little in imagining the narrative involving Seneca and Lucius.

As far as my human helpers, it takes a village, as they say. I am in debt to my readers: Susan Toscani, Lori Ann Finn, Margaret Caddy, and my husband, John Wilder. Your willingness to read through the first drafts of word documents on computer screens never fails to astound me. I thank you for your interest, thoroughness, and support.

Once again, thank you to my editor, Laura Ross. You never disappoint in your unerring ability to pluck out a word or a phrase that confounds or makes no sense. Further, you seem to delight in leaving the tall buildings of Manhattan behind and jumping into the exotic places that these stories take you. Last of all, I don't understand how you manage to immerse yourself in characters and stories so completely that you seem to hear their voices as clearly as I. That you do astounds me, each and every time.

Thank you, Sally Shupe. The work of proofreading requires dedication, thoroughness, and consistency, and I appreciate your work.

And last, I must thank Nancy Cleary of Wyatt-MacKenzie Publishing. Once again, I cannot say enough about your skills in design and production. Ever since I first shared the cover we created for *I, Claudia*, I started hearing from folks who could not wait to read it. This partnership has extended now through six books. Are you ready for a seventh? I hope so because next comes *My Name is Saul*.

A Preview of Lin Wilder's
MY NAME IS SAUL

Coming in 2019

PROLOGUE

"Saul. Where is Saul? Come out, come out, we need to see you!"

My sister Esther, thirteen when I was born, never tired of our games. And she could run like the wind, with Ruth, Bathsheba, Hagar, and Miryam trailing behind her.

"Is that you?"

She was looking behind a sand dune at the beach, knowing full well I was not hiding there.

Louder, she called, "Saul! Where are you?"

The giggling of my sisters grew more and more breathless as they ran through the pure white sand and stood beside the dune that Esther had raced past ten minutes before, pretending she had not seen my tiny three-year-old body.

"I'm here, Esther! Here I am!"

"Saul, I was so worried!" With that, my tall, elegant sister plucked me off the beach to twirl and dance me across the sand. She tried and failed to keep her balance as our small sisters joined in the dance until finally, all five of us collapsed into the laughter that can only emanate from children: pure, musical, pristine. We were ready to return home to lunch, and the loud complaints of our mother.

Sand...always, it was about the sand. "Esther Mordecai House of Benjamin! Soon you will regret the towers of sand you bring into this house for your poor old mother to sweep up!" But

257

Mother could not hide her smile or suppress the signs of mirth in her eyes. That smile, that laughter would be extinguished in just three years.

My name is Saul. In Hebrew, it means *asked for... inquired by God.* Because we are Roman citizens, I was given a second name, but I will never use it: Paul. When my father named me Saul, he encumbered me with expectation. We are born of the Tribe of Benjamin, one of the Twelve Tribes of Israel, and I am named after the youngest son of the Patriarch Jacob and his wife, Rachel.

At six years of age, I was sent to the Jerusalem Temple to study the Law under Gamaliel. This was a privilege offered to no other boy, and one that cost my father dearly, for I was the only son, the youngest of five. In my dreams, I hear the howls of my mother, as my father and I climb the steps of the carriage to make the three-week trek from Tarsus to Jerusalem. Her laments never ceased until her death six months later.

I knew not to cry. I worked to welcome the pain I felt as her wails faded into the distance. I watched my father's expressionless face as the snow-covered mountains of Tarsus disappeared into the background. I forced myself to block the happy memories of being chased by my sisters through the lush southern meadows to the shores of the Mediterranean...the sheer delight and joy of hiding and then being found. As if reading my mind, Father frowned and recited a passage from Habbakuk:

Then the LORD answered me and said,
"Record the vision
And inscribe it on tablets,
That the one who reads it may run.
For the vision is yet for the appointed time;
It hastens toward the goal and it will not fail.
Though it tarries, wait for it;
For it will certainly come, it will not delay.
Behold, as for the proud one,

His soul is not right within him;
But the righteous will live by his faith.
Furthermore, wine betrays the haughty man,
So that he does not stay at home.
He enlarges his appetite like Sheol,
And he is like death, never satisfied.
He also gathers to himself all nations
And collects to himself all peoples.

Now, at the age of twenty-seven, occasionally those memories of what that small boy felt as he left the loving embrace of his mother come back to haunt me. For just a moment, I wonder if he knew that he would never again feel the softness of a woman's lips, breast, and touch. But then I regain control of my wandering thoughts. I cast such foolish and childish sentiments at the feet of the Name Above Every Other, the God of Abraham, Isaac, and Jacob.

The High Priest and the Council of Sanhedrins have given me letters empowering me to enter the houses of believers and arrest them. They are worse than fools, these ignorant followers of the man called Jesus—this weak carpenter from Nazareth, this powerless man who permitted himself to suffer the death of a criminal, crucified on a Roman cross. They claim that he is the Messiah, but he is merely another of the long list of fakers.

The time I was born for is here. I will wage war against these Christians, and I will emerge <u>victorious</u>.

My name is Saul.

CPSIA information can be obtained
at www.ICGtesting.com
Printed in the USA
LVHW031508300719
625872LV00002B/196

9 781948 018432